Sin City Nurses

To have and to fold...

Welcome to Las Vegas, the desert metropolis famous for its lavish nights under skies of dazzling light—but everyone knows Sin City's brightest are found within the walls of its hospitals! Highly professional and always prepared, Las Vegas's fearless nurses can handle anything. But when Cupid's arrow strikes, will they be ready to walk down the aisle?

Find out in

Surgeon's Second Time Lucky

Available now!

And look out for Jasmine and Wyatt's story.

Coming soon!

Dear Reader,

One of the great things about writing is being able to set a story anywhere in the world. Las Vegas has always been on my bucket list, though it might prove dangerous for my bank account. Seeing it through the eyes of Ruby and Harrison, my estranged couple, proved a safer option.

I hope the bright lights and temptations in Sin City are as fun for you to read about as they were to write!

Enjoy!

Karin xx

SURGEON'S SECOND TIME LUCKY

KARIN BAINE

MEDICAL ROMANCE

Recycling programs for this product may not exist in your area

ISBN-13: 978-1-335-99373-1

Surgeon's Second Time Lucky

For questions and comments about the quality of this book, please contact us at CustomerService@Harlequin.com.

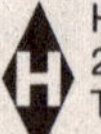

Harlequin Enterprises ULC
22 Adelaide St. West, 41st Floor
Toronto, Ontario M5H 4E3, Canada
www.Harlequin.com

HarperCollins Publishers
Macken House, 39/40 Mayor Street Uppe
Dublin 1, D01 C9W8, Ireland
www.HarperCollins.com

Printed in U.S.A.

1 2 3 4 5 6 7 8 9 10 HDC 28 27 26 25

Karin Baine lives in Northern Ireland with her husband, two sons and her out-of-control notebook collection. Her mother and her grandmother's vast collection of books inspired her love of reading and her dream of becoming a Harlequin author. Now she can tell people she has a proper job! You can follow Karin on X @karinbaine1 or visit her website for the latest news, karinbaine.com.

Books by Karin Baine

Harlequin Medical Romance

Christmas North and South

Festive Fling with the Surgeon

Jet Set Docs

Spanish Doc to Heal Her

Royal York Hospital

Winter Nights with the Midwife

Nurse's New Year with the Billionaire
Tempted by Her Off-Limits Boss
A Nurse, a Pup, a Second Chance

Harlequin Romance

Princesses' Night Out

Temptation in a Tiara

A Pact Between Tycoons

The Trouble with Italian Millionaires

Cinderella's Festive Fake Date
The Tycoon's Festive Houseguest

Visit the Author Profile page
at Harlequin.com for more titles.

For Sheila xx

CHAPTER ONE

'I've never seen anything like this in Las Vegas.' Nurse Ruby Jones watched as the casualties were wheeled into Clover Hospital. Paramedics shouting to be heard over the hubbub of the walking wounded to get help for the most seriously injured on the stretchers.

'It's all hands on deck tonight. A gas explosion means not only burns, but crush injuries from falling debris and collapsed buildings.' Nell, one of the doctors in the department, wrapped her stethoscope around her neck, then rushed over to assign herself to one of the patients being stretchered in.

Ruby took a deep breath and did the same. In major incidents like this the patients were assessed as they came in with the most urgent cases treated as soon as possible. The emergency department was ground zero and it looked, and felt, like a battleground.

People filling every available space were

clutching damaged body parts. The once pristine bright corridors now splattered with blood and debris from those staggering in off the street. The air was thick with the smell of smoke, drifting in through the open doors. Even the noise was almost unbearable. The injured screaming and crying in pain. Medical staff shouting to be heard trying to treat the patients. It was overwhelming. Claustrophobic. Frightening. Yet there was no room for thoughts of herself when people's lives were literally in her hands.

Ruby worked quickly and efficiently helping to assess the injured and prioritise the most serious cases.

The sight of a little boy seriously burned stopped her in her tracks. So small and vulnerable, he immediately pulled at her heartstrings. He couldn't be any older than her daughter, Aimee. Who, thankfully, was at home being fussed over by her grandmother. Safe.

'Ten-year-old boy, Eugene Collins. He was in the apartment block where the explosion happened and found under the rubble. Extensive second-degree burns, crush injuries to the abdomen. Unresponsive at the scene.' Wyatt Logan, one of the paramedics she saw regularly in the emergency department, reeled off the boy's injuries and the treatment he'd been given since. Now it was down to Ruby and her colleagues to make sure he came through this.

'Okay, let's get an IV set up and oxygen started,' Nell instructed the medical team as they transferred the boy from the stretcher.

It was hard to look at the small body, covered in soot and dirt, raw wounds needing attention. But this was Ruby's job. To save lives. She could get emotional later once she knew little Eugene was stable.

As expected, Nell's preliminary exam determined that along with his other injuries, he was suffering from smoke inhalation. His lungs struggling, and his throat swollen, making breathing difficult. 'I'm going to intubate him to help him breathe, then we'll look at those burns.'

They inserted the plastic tube down his throat to assist with the boy's breathing, and Ruby wondered what had happened to his parents. If they were being treated elsewhere in the department, or if he'd been orphaned by the blast.

Her heart broke for the child. Aimee's dad hadn't wanted to stick around the moment he knew he was going to be a father, but at least she had a mother to care for her. There had been no way Ruby was going to let the chance of being a mother slip through her hands again. Not after losing a baby at the age of eighteen.

A trauma which not only devastated her but showed the cracks in her fledgling marriage. She and Harrison had been high school sweethearts and their future plans for marriage had been pushed forward with the discovery that she was pregnant. Her new husband working and studying hard to give their family a home and the best start.

In hindsight, they had been too young to fully understand the commitment they'd been making. Or, at least, Harrison had been. Proving he was too immature to deal with the emotional complications of a miscarriage. Grief had driven Ruby back home to her parents, but Harrison hadn't followed her. The separation, combined with the loss of the baby, had driven them apart permanently. Eventually, she'd returned to her studies and qualified as a nurse, plunging all of her energy into her career.

Then, four years later, she'd met Chad. She'd thought she'd met the real 'one.' The pregnancy hadn't been planned but that was no excuse for his behaviour. In the end, he'd done a runner, leaving her as a single parent. She only managed to juggle her career with raising Aimee because she had her parents' help. Hopefully, Eugene would have the same level of family support to get him through this traumatic time.

'We have a new burns specialist transferred

from St Michael's in Boulder City. I'll give him a call,' Nell suggested.

'You would think with the scale of this emergency he would have checked in already.' It irked her that someone so clearly needed on a night like this wouldn't step up simply because they weren't rostered on. As far as she was concerned, being a medical professional wasn't just a job, it was a vocation. More than a paycheck, this was about saving lives, and those who didn't think about that first weren't right for the job, in her opinion.

'Sorry about that. I got caught up helping with the injured out on the street. I'm Dr Blake, the new burns specialist. Now, where do you need me?' It was the voice behind her which sent chills along the back of her neck, before she turned around to face him.

Time had chiseled his features into that of a handsome, mature man, from the teen she had known, but the swoop of dark hair, deep brown eyes and full smile hadn't changed that much. Harrison. Her ex-husband. Father to the baby she'd lost. The love of her life who hadn't loved her enough to stay. And now he was here, in front of her.

It took a moment for Ruby to compose herself, not wanting to give away the nature of the relationship they'd once had to any of her colleagues. No one here knew of her life before she'd qualified as a nurse, and that was the way she wanted to keep it. Especially if she and Harrison were apparently going to be working in the same hospital from now on.

She saw the moment too when he recognized her, the almost imperceptible sharp intake of breath, and flare of recognition in his eyes. Before he could say anything which might have given away their secret, Ruby jumped in.

'Here. For the boy, I mean. He will have to get an X-ray to see what internal damage there might be, but he's suffered some serious burns over his body.' She was doing her best not to appear flustered, maintaining her professional demeanor, even though her heart was beating so fast it felt as if she'd just run a marathon.

He'd always had this effect on her. It didn't matter that they'd grown up together in high school and she'd seen him practically every day, he'd always made her heart race. Her body apparently hadn't processed the fact he'd abandoned her when she'd needed him most. Traitor.

Harrison looked at her for a moment as though there was something he wanted to say. A blink, and it was gone as he turned his attention to the young boy on the bed. She couldn't help but wonder what was going on in his mind. Regret? Nostalgia? A wish to be anywhere else than here near her? Ruby supposed she'd never know, but she had a million questions of her own running around her head. All based around what he'd been doing for the past fifteen years, and why he hadn't come back for her.

But he wasn't here for her now either.

'I won't know exactly what we're dealing with until we're able to clean and debride the wounds, removing any dead tissue. At a glance, I'm afraid he's going to need skin grafts.' Harrison frowned. 'It's going to be a long road back to recovery.'

'As long as he does recover. We'll have to keep him sedated and give him pain relief until we're able to patch him up properly.' With those sorts of wounds, the little boy would be in a serious amount of pain otherwise. At least whilst he was asleep, he might be spared the worst of it. Ruby brushed the matted dark hair from Eugene's brow. The children were always the most difficult for her to deal with.

Not only did they make her think of her own daughter in serious jeopardy, but also of the child she'd lost. Harrison here beside her amplified that feeling of loss. Wondering if their child would have been a little dark-haired boy like his father, or fair like his mother. Aimee took after her with her long blond hair and blue eyes. Thankfully she didn't look anything like her ex, so there was no permanent reminder of the other man who'd let her down so spectacularly.

When Ruby glanced up, Harrison was watching the interaction intently and she wondered if he was thinking about the child they'd never been given the chance to parent. Probably not, since once his responsibility was over, he'd disappeared from her life altogether. Until now.

'I'll do my best for him, Ruby. You know I will.' He gave her that devastating smile she'd forgotten could wreak so much havoc on her insides.

'I know.' Although she hadn't seen him in so long or witnessed him in action as a fully qualified medical professional until now, she was sure he cared about each and every patient. He'd always had a good heart. That was why it had been so hard to come to terms with the way things had ended between them. Cold and completely unlike the man she'd known and loved.

Ruby caught the other members of staff glancing between them, probably bemused by the familiarity between them when they were supposed to be recently introduced strangers.

'Yes, well, welcome to the hospital, Dr Blake. Once we get Eugene stabilized we'll get you back to take a look at the burns. Perhaps in the meantime you could check on the other patients and see what you can do for them too.' Ruby made sure to put that distinction back in their roles here. They had much to discuss, and though she didn't know if it would happen, or even if she wanted it to, that conversation needed to take place outside of a busy emergency department.

'Of course, Nurse…' he took a look at her name tag but didn't bat an eyelid when he saw she'd reverted to her maiden name, 'Jones. Although, I'm sure we'll be seeing a lot of each other in the future.' The twinkle in Harrison's eyes as he said it let her know that he wasn't just talking about meeting in a professional capacity.

The thought of it, of being alone with Harrison Blake, the love of her life, was something she knew she wasn't going to stop thinking about for the foreseeable future. With their painful history, it shouldn't be something she was looking forward to either, but she was. If only to give him a piece of her mind and get some closure. At least, that's what she was telling herself.

Seeing Ruby again out of the blue made Harrison feel as though someone had just delivered two thousand volts of electricity to his heart. She was the last person he'd expected to run into here. If he'd known, he mightn't have entertained the idea of a transfer from Boulder City, never mind moving. This was supposed to mark a change in his life. Moving forward. Not having to face the past. Especially when it had taken so long to get over what had happened to him and Ruby, and the grief he'd carried with him for so long. Now it seemed he was going to have to confront it all over again.

It was always going to be difficult facing her again. That's why he'd avoided it for so long. Until things were so broken between them there was no way to fix things again. Of course they were different people now, with different lives. Virtual strangers, but with a history he doubted either of them had ever been fully able to forget.

That meant finally telling her why he hadn't been able to comfort her, to be the husband she'd needed. Because losing the baby had destroyed him too. It had reopened old wounds. Reminding him of when his big brother had died. His hero. His world. They'd call it post-traumatic stress disorder these days. He hadn't understood at the time. Thought he was being selfish in wallowing in his own misery and that Ruby would be better off without him. She was young enough to start her life over again and forget about him, along with the child they'd never know.

It had taken a decline in his mental health and subsequent recovery for him to realise he'd been wrong, but by that time it was too late. He had no choice other than to try and move on too by finishing medical school and becoming the doctor he was now. Finding out that Ruby had completed her nursing the way they'd always planned was a surprise, but he was nonetheless proud of her.

In that moment of seeing her again, recognizing her despite the sleeker blond mane and more angular features than he remembered, he'd been transported to his teenage self. That instant flare of attraction before regret and guilt had set in for how things had ended between them. His love for her had never died, but he'd let it all slip away in the haze of depression and grief which had consumed him for too long. Making him weak and vulnerable and barely able to function, never mind be a good husband. Hopefully he'd get the chance to try and put things right, even if he could never hope to make amends or reconnect with the only woman he'd ever truly loved. That time might have passed. Unfortunately.

He could see Ruby out of the corner of his eye, rushing between patients and taking care of everyone. If this was her as a nurse, he could only imagine the mother she would have made to their baby. As always, the thought brought sadness with it. That feeling of loss and what could have been.

He guessed he'd never know because since then he'd made sure never to put himself in that vulnerable position again. No one else had ever claimed a piece of his heart the way Ruby had because he didn't stick around long enough for that to happen. As for ideas of a family, that notion had been well and truly quashed. He could never go through that kind of grief again. So, he'd lived the bachelor life, casual relationships a low priority next to his work.

Now, however, his personal life and his professional one were about to collide spectacularly. With such emotional ties to Ruby already, he had no idea how things were going to pan out. He only hoped neither of them would get hurt again along the way.

CHAPTER TWO

RUBY HAD BEEN aware of Harrison's presence all night. She knew the rest of the staff were pleased to have him on board, advising on the more seriously burned patients, and in most cases, taking over their care. Treating them personally and showing a compassion for all. It was difficult not to ask herself why he hadn't been able to do that for her when she'd desperately needed his support.

'I'm glad things have begun to calm down. Hopefully we'll get back to the usual status quo where all we have to deal with is the aftermath of drunken confrontations and tourists who've had too much sun.' Nell was yawning, reminding her that it had been a long night. An emotional one too, for various reasons.

'There's never a dull moment, is there?' That had been part of the attraction for Ruby. Always keeping her too busy to dwell on the past. Working somewhere that made her feel needed, appreciated, less lonely. She hadn't accounted for ending up as a single mother along the way. Aimee satisfied all of those criteria for her too. Ruby had been born to be a mother as much as a nurse. It was simply a shame she'd had to experience so much trauma before finally getting there.

'We'd worry if there was,' her colleague chirped much too heartily for the time of morning, apparently getting a new wind as she lifted a new patient file from the desk.

Ruby, on the other hand, was beginning to feel the strain of being on her feet all night and into the next morning. She rubbed at the back of her neck absentmindedly, looking forward to spending the rest of the day in bed whilst Aimee was at school. Thank goodness for doting grandparents who were able to mind her overnight when her mother was working night shifts.

'You only feel it when you stop, don't you?' Harrison appeared beside her, furthering the tension already in her body.

'I didn't know you were still here, Dr Blake.'

'I'm just about to leave. I have to say, it was quite the introduction. Not how I imagined spending my first shift here.' He was smiling, doing his best to make things easy between them, but Ruby couldn't help but bristle every time he was near.

'Strictly speaking, this isn't your department, but we appreciate you helping out.' It was her attempt to put him in his place and make sure he was under no allusion that they were going to be friends. That would be too much to ask of her when he'd broken her heart and walked away, leaving her to deal with her grief all on her own. She wasn't going to simply forgive and forget because he was back in her life and wanted to carry on as though nothing had happened.

'Ruby, we don't have to keep pretending. There's no one around to hear. I think we need to talk.' Harrison took her hand, and though he was gentle with her, she was trembling nonetheless.

'I don't think so. Fifteen years ago was the time to do that.' She snatched her hand away again.

'Please, hear me out. If we're going to be working together in future, it's important that I explain things to you.'

'I don't want to hear it.' Ruby didn't want to be drawn back into memories of that time. It was still too painful to revisit.

'Please.' If he'd said anything else, looked at her with anything other than pain in his eyes, she wouldn't even have considered relenting. However, that same hurt she felt every day remembering their past was so evident in Harrison she'd be heartless to ignore it. Besides, he was right. She couldn't work here, seeing him all the time, and not address it. If she didn't get some kind of closure, it was going to open that wound every time their paths crossed.

However, she was too weary, too emotionally exhausted by the night's events to take this on now. She needed time to build her defences back up before confronting their painful past. A good sleep, some food and some time to think over the implications of having Harrison back in her life were needed before that conversation. Not necessarily in that order.

At the very least, he might tell her some things she wasn't ready to hear. That he hadn't loved her. That losing their baby had been for the best. That he'd met someone else. Any of those scenarios would crush her when she was already feeling vulnerable at being ambushed here at work by him.

She huffed out a sigh as she faced the inevitable. 'Fine, but not here, not now. I'm going to need some time.'

He looked relieved. As though she'd taken a load off his shoulders. A guilty conscience, perhaps? Good. He should feel bad about leaving her to grieve on her own the way he had.

See? That's exactly why she needed a little time and space. Otherwise she'd end up lashing out.

Harrison held his hands up. 'Of course. Sorry. This has come as a shock to me too.'

Ruby supposed seeing one another again like this must have been hard for him too. Albeit for different reasons. Being confronted by a painful past wasn't easy for anyone.

'You must have considered it a possibility when you moved here?' Okay, so he would never have known she was a nurse, or that she'd be working here, but Spring Valley, their hometown wasn't that far away. The last place he'd known her to be.

'It crossed my mind, but it's a big city. I thought the chances were slim.' Otherwise he might never have considered the move…she could read between the lines.

It wasn't a surprise that he never had any intention of seeking her out, accepting responsibility for the hurt he'd caused. Not when he'd been content to leave her on her own so soon after the miscarriage.

'Sorry to disappoint you.' She wasn't. He deserved his comeuppance in having to face his failure as a husband.

His sudden smile was alarming in the circumstances. 'Are you kidding? I'm so proud of you. Thankful that you finished your studies too and became the nurse I always knew you could be.'

If it had come from anyone else, the sentiment could have been construed as patronizing, or condescending. Except Ruby knew he meant it. They'd spent so long discussing their dream careers, and worked hard to achieve them, until circumstances had steered life in another direction. With her doubting herself every step of the way, and Harrison championing her. In completing her studies, and qualifying, it had felt as though she was showing him she could do it without him. Deep down knowing he'd want it for her, regardless of what had gone on between them.

That didn't mean she was going to make this easy for him when she'd been carrying this burden of rejection, abandonment, and feeling of not being good enough for so long, thanks to Harrison.

'Well, it was either that, or carry on haunting my parents' house like some wailing ghost of an abandoned wife who couldn't move on from the past.'

She had a lot of sympathy with those spectral figures rumoured to haunt old buildings, replaying traumatic events forevermore. It had been incredibly hard to pick herself up and start over, but there had always been that sense of having unfinished business as well as the sense of injustice. If nothing else, perhaps seeing Harrison again would finally give her that closure she didn't get first time around.

The flicker of shame which crossed his face gave her some satisfaction. He should feel ashamed of what he'd been able to do to someone he'd professed to love forever.

'I'm sorry. Of course I didn't expect you to sit around waiting for me, or my approval. I just… yeah… I'm glad you're doing well.' The half-smile could have weakened another woman. One who hadn't been fooled by this handsome man before into thinking he cared. But Ruby was a little older, wiser and more cynical to take him at face value anymore.

He was likely just trying to make his own life easier by trying to get her onside rather than being confronted by a still furious ex-wife. Which, as of right now, she still was. This wasn't simply about a bad teenage break-up she should have just got over. It had been the most traumatic time of her life. A mixture of grief and loss compounded by Harrison's betrayal of her trust and the subsequent dissolution of their marriage.

A smile, no matter how endearing, was not going to get him off the hook.

'I am. Now. However, it did take time to pick myself up again after everything that happened. Once I realized that I was on my own.'

Ruby didn't want to be impressed by him, or think about how handsome he looked, even more so now. The only emotion she wanted to associate with Harrison Blake was hate. She'd even take blind rage. Anything except liking him, because she needed closure. A reason to put him from her thoughts forever. Once she knew exactly why he'd abandoned her she could hopefully put it all behind her and finally move on.

Ruby was certain that Chad had been her second mistake because she'd been desperate to replace Harrison in her life. Perhaps he'd felt that she didn't truly love him and he'd seen the pregnancy as an excuse to leave. Although she'd been content these past years with just her and Aimee, it might not be such a bad thing to finally close this particularly painful chapter of her life.

'I know nothing can excuse my actions, but I would like a chance to explain myself, Ruby. I've just moved into a new house nearby. Perhaps we could have a chat there after work.' Harrison's suggestion, regardless of her curiosity about what he had to say to her, was still a little too much too soon for Ruby. She wasn't sure she was ready for whatever he had to say.

'If I was prepared to hear you out, I'd prefer to have that conversation somewhere more neutral.' And public. She knew nothing about this man anymore, and being alone with him, on his own turf was a step too far. Although, it was possible he had a wife and children at home and it might not be just the two of them. A notion that didn't sit well with her either.

How would she feel if she found out he'd gone on to father another child with someone else? Being supportive to another wife and leaving her behind would be a double betrayal.

'Okay. You decide and let me know. It's on your terms, Ruby.' He sounded sincere, as if he actually cared about how she felt and what she wanted. Which only made the memories of those days and nights, spent sobbing for the loss of her husband and baby, hurt even more. Wondering why he couldn't come to her. Hug her and tell her everything was going to be okay the way he usually did when she'd needed his support.

'I'll let you know,' she said, making no firm commitment. Not knowing if she'd ever be ready to have that discussion, but hoping that would be enough to drop the subject for now.

At least until she got her head around the situation and came to terms with the fact Harrison was back in her life. If even on the periphery.

He nodded, and finally walked away from the nurses' station, apparently content with the small concession. Ruby couldn't help but wonder if this unexpected run-in would have as much impact on him as it was already having on her. It was clear that he'd never wanted, or intended, to see her again. She had thought about it over the years, and how she'd react to seeing him again. In her mind she'd blasted him over how selfish he'd been, cursed the day she'd ever met him. All the while suspecting she'd end up a sobbing mess because despite everything she'd loved him.

This low key interaction wasn't what she'd expected. She put it down to the fact she was at work, and they'd been dealing with a large-scale emergency. Trying not to think about the other emotions she'd never dreamed she'd have upon seeing him again. Like thinking about how much she'd missed him. Or how her heart still skipped a beat every time she looked at him.

Ruby shook her head. She needed to get out of here and clear him out of her thoughts altogether. Hopefully their paths wouldn't cross again until she was better emotionally equipped to deal with him again.

She was just about to pass on her nightly report to the next shift when she caught sight of her mother rushing in through the doors of the emergency department, carrying a near hysterical Aimee in her arms. Her heart dropped into the bottom of her stomach.

'What is it? What happened?' She ran over, immediately searching her daughter for signs of injury.

'I'm so sorry, Ruby. I only took my eyes off her for a moment...' Her mother was clearly in shock too, her face pale and eyes wide with panic.

'What happened?' she asked again, reaching for Aimee.

The little girl wrapped her arms around her mother's neck, transferring between the two women, and clinging to her like a baby koala.

It was then Ruby saw the bandage on Aimee's arm.

'She said she wanted to make me breakfast. The coffee went all over her. I'm so sorry. I tried running her arm under the cold water but she was screaming. Your father's at work so I thought it best to bring her down here.' Ruby's mother was babbling, but she could just about make out what had happened.

'Why didn't you call me?' she asked, whisking her daughter to an empty cubicle so she could get a better look at her injury.

'I tried, but it just kept going to your voicemail. I thought it would be quicker to bring her down.' It was only now Ruby could see that her mother was in her pyjamas and slippers under her overcoat, and had obviously driven here in a hurry.

'Sorry.' Ruby pulled her phone from her pocket to see that she'd turned it off and forgotten to turn it back on. 'We had an emergency with the gas explosion.'

'I heard about that on the news. I hope everyone is okay.' Her mother took a seat whilst Ruby set Aimee down on the gurney and began to unwrap her arm.

'I don't know the full extent of the damage yet, but we were full overnight. That's why I'm just getting off now.' If she'd left on time she might have been able to prevent this, but Ruby could never promise a set time when she had a duty here to her patients. Sometimes though, she wondered if she was compromising her role as a mother in the process. It wasn't easy being the only parent in her daughter's life and she often thought about whether or not Aimee was suffering as a result. This morning the answer was a resounding 'yes,' and impossible for Ruby not to feel guilty over it.

'Now, baby girl, Mommy's going to take a look at your arm and fix it all up, okay?' Ruby carefully peeled away the dressing her mother had placed on the wound, doing her best not to react to the angry red burn marring her daughter's otherwise smooth skin. At least Aimee's heart-piercing cries had dwindled down to a whimper as she sniffed through her tears. Hopefully, it was a reaction to the shock rather than the actual pain.

'Is everything okay in here, Nurse Jones? I saw you rushing in here.' A concerned-looking Harrison stepped into the cubicle, assessing the scene before him.

Great. This was all she needed. Her life now spectacularly clashing with the past.

Ruby's mother and Harrison exchanged glances, and she held her breath as recognition and confusion registered on their faces.

'Mommy, it hurts.' Aimee drew everyone's attention back to her as she dissolved into pitiful tears. It was all Ruby could do not to sweep her up into her arms, but she needed to treat the wound before it became infected. There would be time for cuddles and treats once they got home.

'I know, sweetheart, and I'm going to make

it all better for you.' Ruby could feel Harrison's eyes glaring into the back of her head. If it was a shock seeing her again, finding out she had a daughter would be a double whammy. Though she didn't owe him anything, she wished she could have broken the news a little easier. Certainly, if she'd discovered he'd had children after they'd lost their baby, it would have come as a gut punch to her. Then again, he hadn't seemed to be too overwrought at the time…

Harrison cleared his throat. If he had something to say, or questions to ask about her family, it appeared he was going to save them for now. 'Is there anything I can do?'

'I don't think we need your help,' Ruby's mother snapped.

Ruby had forgotten she wasn't the only one to bear a grudge over the way things had ended. After all, it was her parents who'd had to mop up her tears and prop her up again when the divorce was finalized and he'd decided to stay out of her life on a permanent basis.

'Mom. This is Dr Blake. He's just transferred here as a burns specialist so he's the right person to be here.' Ruby hoped the warning look she shot her mother was enough to quieten her for now. Aimee took priority over everything. Including old wounds.

Her mother grumped as she folded her arms, but put up no further resistance.

'May I?' Harrison looked to Ruby for approval to approach Aimee and she nodded.

He crouched down so he was eye level with Aimee. 'I'm Harrison. What's your name?'

'Aimee.' Her daughter watched him through lowered lashes, already enamoured with the handsome doctor.

Ruby sighed. Apparently her offspring's taste in men was as ill-judged as her own.

'Well, Aimee, I'm just going to take a look at your arm if that's okay? Then your mother and I will try and make it all better.'

Aimee bit her bottom lip and nodded. She wasn't a child who trusted easily and it said a lot about Harrison that she was letting him intervene without a fuss. Though, as far as Ruby was concerned, it only proved he was only someone who could be trusted short-term. Any sort of long-term, emotional commitment, was apparently beyond the man, as she'd found out to her cost. A distinction she wanted to keep hold of even all this time later so she didn't forget what he'd put her through, regardless of who he might be these days.

Harrison gently cleaned the wound, murmuring soothing words anytime Aimee flinched. Ruby sat down beside her and took her other hand to offer some comfort whilst Harrison assessed the extent of the burn. Although she'd dealt with this kind of injury on many occasions herself, it wouldn't hurt to have an expert's opinion. Especially if it meant limiting any permanent damage or scarring to her daughter's skin.

'Well?' Her mother's impatience got the better of her.

'I'd say what we're dealing with here is a partial thickness burn, so it shouldn't leave any permanent scarring.' He smiled at Aimee. 'That doesn't mean it isn't painful. I'm going to put a dressing on it and give you some pain relief, Aimee. It might get itchy, but try not to scratch and make it worse. Mom can put some emollient on it so the skin doesn't get too dry.'

Ruby sighed out her relief. It was good to get a second opinion when it was her own loved one she was dealing with. 'Thanks, Harrison.'

She watched as he carefully dressed the affected area, by which time Aimee's tears had dried up altogether. A dramatic end to an arduous shift. Ruby was physically and emotionally drained.

'I think Miss Aimee deserves some ice cream for being so brave.' Harrison ruffled her daughter's hair. It was surreal watching the interaction, but also made Ruby think about the child they'd lost, and what kind of father he would have made. It was difficult to tell when he seemed so involved here, yet had disappeared out of her life completely once he was off the hook.

'Mommy?' Aimee looked at her with pleading eyes that she could never say no to.

'I guess there's no school for you today, anyway.' They were both going to need some sleep after everything that had happened.

'Don't expect me to babysit. I have to go to work myself. I'm going to be late as it is. Thank goodness I've got a clean uniform in my locker at the store or I'd be in real trouble.' Her mother was gathering her things, and Ruby couldn't blame her for being upset in the circumstances. Hopefully they'd get to have a chat later and she could smooth her ruffled feathers.

'Thanks for bringing her in, Mom. Can you give us a lift home before you start?' Ruby was looking forward to falling into bed, and hoping Aimee would do the same for a while at least.

'I'm sorry, Ruby. I told you, I'm already late. You'll have to take a cab. I'll see you later, Aimee Bear.' Her mother dropped a kiss on Aimee's head before disappearing out of the cubicle and leaving Ruby open-mouthed.

She really didn't relish the thought of trying

to get her injured daughter onto a bus or a cab at this time of the day.

'I can give you a lift if you want?' Harrison's offer was generous and unexpected. Even if it did present a new dilemma. As much as she wanted to get home as soon as possible, she didn't want him to think this was any kind of reconciliation. An acceptance that all was forgiven. Far from it.

'Then we can all get ice cream!' Aimee's injury was forgotten at the exciting prospect, making it even more difficult for Ruby to wriggle out of this. She didn't want to upset her daughter any more than she already was. Even though Harrison didn't deserve any sort of second chance with her, Ruby had to put Aimee's happiness before her own.

'For breakfast?' she asked in a last-ditch attempt to get everyone to see sense.

'Why not? Ice cream is an anytime food as far as I'm concerned.' Harrison grinned at her.

Ruby should have known better than to challenge his sweet tooth. This was someone who'd insisted on celebrating every occasion with sweet treats. It was a wonder he wasn't the size of a house by now. He must really look after himself to be in such good shape.

When she realized she was trying to assess

the body beneath the lab coat, she had to admit defeat. ‘Fine. Ice cream for breakfast it is.’

‘Yay.’ Aimee high-fived Harrison with her good arm and Ruby got the distinct impression that there was more than her waistline in trouble with this new alliance.

CHAPTER THREE

'WHY DON'T YOU go and help yourself to some toppings. If that's okay with your mom?' Too late, Harrison looked to Ruby for approval, suddenly aware that he might have overstepped the mark.

'I guess so,' Ruby said through thinned lips, and Harrison knew he'd messed up. Again.

Sorry, he mouthed to her, as a happy Aimee skipped over to the topping station with her bowl of ice cream.

'That's all right, I'll send her home with you so you can watch her bouncing off the walls on her sugar high later.' There was a hint of a smile playing on Ruby's mouth now so he was able to relax a little, even though this was a strange situation for both of them.

'I'm not used to being around children outside of the hospital, where ice cream is always the answer. I don't stick around for the consequences.' His choice of words drew raised eyebrows from Ruby and he knew exactly why. As far as she knew, once they'd lost their baby he'd disappeared from her life, because he'd never explained why. Perhaps if he'd been able to express his feelings of loss and grief, and how they'd overwhelmed him, they might have been able to save their marriage. Easy to say in hindsight, but he'd never really know because he'd internalized everything until it had destroyed him, along with their relationship.

'I'm sure the parents love you,' Ruby muttered, taking a sip of coffee. The adults having opted for caffeine over sugar after their long night.

'Well, the young patients do at least.' Although they were glossing over the obvious elephant in the diner, Harrison was also struggling with finding out that Ruby had become a mother after all. He supposed he shouldn't have been surprised, given how happy she'd been when they'd discovered they were going to be parents, regardless that it hadn't been a planned pregnancy. And how devastated she'd been too after the miscarriage.

He was happy for her, Aimee was a lovely little girl. But he was also sad that he'd never got to see their baby grow up. It had been too early in the pregnancy to even know if it would have been a son or daughter when she'd still been in her first trimester. Not that it would have mattered, but that loss had ensured he'd never get the chance to be a father. He couldn't handle losing another loved one. So once a relationship seemed as though it was getting serious, he backed away. Before he ended up getting hurt again.

'I think Aimee's a fan already. She's hardly bothered by her arm at all since you appeared, even though I just lost a couple of years off my life through the stress.'

'There's always ice cream to make you feel better. You can have anything you want. It's my treat.'

'I'm good with the coffee, thanks. I'll take an IV full of it if you're offering,' Ruby said with a yawn.

Despite the playful back-and-forth, there was an awkwardness between them which grew as they slipped into silence. Both watching Aimee scoop candies and sprinkles onto her breakfast ice cream, and hoping she'd return to the table soon.

The owner, who'd been surprised at having customers asking for ice cream so early in the morning, until they'd explained what had happened, was currently plying Aimee with crayons and colouring books. The middle-aged woman clearly felt sorry for the little blonde girl in her pyjamas who'd been in the wars and had a large dressing on her arm to prove it.

'She looks like you.' Harrison said it without thinking. He had no clue what Aimee's father looked like, but the resemblance to Ruby was uncanny. The blond hair, blue eyes and even the little dimple at the corner of her mouth when she smiled.

It was visible now in her mother. 'Yeah. She hasn't inherited much from her father, thank goodness.'

'Oh?' His curiosity was piqued. Of course he'd been interested to know who Aimee's father was but it hadn't seemed appropriate to ask. Harrison had no right to know anything about Ruby's life since their split, but it did appear as though the relationship hadn't ended well.

'Yeah. Turned out he wasn't the man I thought he was either.' It was a thinly veiled dig which Harrison couldn't begrudge her when he knew how badly he'd let her down. He had hoped that she would have found happiness with someone, even if it hadn't been with him.

'I'm sorry. I didn't know you'd remarried.'

'I didn't. Aimee hadn't been planned and fatherhood proved a commitment too far for Chad. What about you? Have you got a wife or kids?'

He shook his head. How did he ever begin

to explain why not? Therapy had shown him how important it was to talk, to open up and not keep things to himself, so not having the chance to explain to Ruby why things had ended the way they had was killing him.

'Listen, Ruby, I know I said I'd wait until you were ready, but I really need to talk about what happened between us.' All he needed was a chance to finally give her some answers, and then perhaps it mightn't be so awkward between them. If they had the opportunity to talk things out, maybe it would make working together a little easier. Even if being with Ruby, seeing her with her daughter, was a reminder of everything he'd lost.

'Harrison…' Before she was able to stop him from saying anything more, Aimee returned to the table and did it for her.

'This is yummy.' Aimee had chocolate sauce all around her face and hands as she spooned some of the sugar-laden breakfast dessert into her mouth.

It wasn't a conversation they could continue now that Aimee was in listening range. Harrison had lost the moment to tell Ruby that it hadn't been her fault, nor had he been a coward and run away. Losing the baby had devastated them both, but he hoped they could still come back from it to be civil with one another, at work at least.

'Don't get too used to it, missy. This is a special treat.' Ruby took a napkin from the table and started wiping her daughter's face.

It was strange to watch their interaction: so natural and endearing, yet painful too. In another life he might have been part of this scene as more than an outsider. Would he have been the one still pushing ice cream for breakfast with their own child, or the strict parent who would want their offspring to grow up on a healthier diet? He had more than a suspicion he would've been the pushover spoiling their little one, leaving Ruby to do the disciplining.

Mostly because that was how his big brother, Joey, had been with him. A ten-year age gap between them meant Harrison was the little brother trailing along after Joey when he wanted to be with friends his own age. Joey could easily have pushed him away, but he'd taken him very much under his wing. Buying Harrison anything he wanted once he got his first job, and treating him to days out and afternoons at the ice cream parlour. That's where he'd learned what it was like to be loved when their parents had been too busy working, trying to keep the family afloat, to pay their sons any real attention.

Harrison was only eleven years old when Joey had been hit by a drunk driver. His life extinguished on one dark, rainy night. He could still hear his mother's screams even now as the police had delivered the news. His own grief had been immeasurable. The void left behind was something he thought could never be filled. Until he'd met Ruby.

After Joey's death, they'd moved house to try and start fresh as a family. Although they'd all been too locked into their individual sadness to ever really come together again. Their parents had divorced a couple of years later, and Harrison had stayed with his mother.

Ruby had been his lifeline. He was the new kid in town, and she'd been appointed in class to show him around and they'd hit it off immediately. Best friends until teenage hormones had made it more. Even fifteen years later, he'd never loved another woman the way he'd loved Ruby Jones.

He'd never told her about his brother. Even now he found it difficult to talk about Joey, because that choking grief crept slowly back to consume him every time he thought of everything his brother had missed out on. His own life without Joey in it. That was why the miscarriage had such an effect on him. He'd been transported back to that all-encompassing feeling of loss, and how life could never be the same again. Worse, he'd been right. Everything he'd known had been taken away from him a second time in the aftermath of a loved one's death.

'Harrison? Are you okay? You seem a little zoned out.' Ruby was watching him intently across the table and he realized he'd been lost in the past. Never a good place for him to visit, though it was understandable after his many shocks over the course of these past few hours.

'Yes. Sorry. I guess everything is just catching up with me.' He drew back from the darkness and into the light of today, where he was having breakfast with Ruby and Aimee. An infinitely more pleasing place to be, regardless of what she might currently think of him.

Ruby nodded towards a drowsy Aimee, whose head was nodding dangerously close to the half-eaten bowl of ice cream, eyes closed and spoon still in hand. 'I think we could all do with going to bed. I mean, going home. Our own homes.'

Harrison smiled as she fumbled her words. The pretty pink tinge to her cheeks a sign that she wasn't as cool, calm and collected as she'd presented thus far. 'I think you're right.'

Ruby extracted the spoon from Aimee's sticky hand and the child turned and clung to her mother as she scooped her up. They made their way back to the car and he had to help extricate Aimee so they could strap her into the back seat.

Again, it struck him how this looked like a typical domestic scene, but one he had no right to be a part of. Aimee wasn't his daughter, and Ruby was no longer his wife. He'd forfeited any opportunity to have some version of this when he'd let her go without a fight. Having this with anyone else was off the table too when the shutters had come down around his heart the second his baby had died.

Harrison got into the front of the car and Ruby sat beside him in the passenger seat.

'Thanks again for doing this, Harrison. I know it's probably the last thing you feel like doing.'

He didn't tell her it was probably the highlight of his week. Despite all the memories of the bad which had come flooding back the moment he'd laid eyes on her again, he was enjoying being part of her life for a short while, and meeting her daughter. Finally finding out what had happened to her after he'd gone from her life.

It was bittersweet to discover that she hadn't been permanently wounded by events. Although he was happy for her that she'd been able to move on, and had her family around her, he was full of regret and sadness that he hadn't managed to achieve the same.

The move here had been an attempt to inject some life into his days, realizing that he'd been stuck in a rut. Focusing on work, and leaving little room for any existence beyond that. He hadn't expected for everything to change all so dramatically, so quickly.

'It's not a problem. You're on my route anyway.' When she gave him her address, he realized Ruby's place wasn't too far from his new house. Only time would tell if that was a good thing or not. He certainly hadn't moved here with the intention of even seeing her again. At least, not consciously.

'I'm sure you're busy with moving in.'

'I've had a few days to settle in. I don't officially start work until tomorrow, remember?' So much for one last relaxing day to do a bit of sightseeing and maybe even a hand of poker at one of the casinos. He'd thought he'd have time to do the tourist thing before becoming a resident, but as usual, life had thrown him a curve ball. At least this time it had brought someone back into his life instead of taking someone else away from him.

'Oh, yes. Welcome to Las Vegas, I guess.' Ruby gave him a bright smile that was still capable of undoing him. In the old days driving together, she would have laid her head on his shoulder and held his free hand in hers. It seemed absurd, not to mention sad, that they were sitting here as strangers now, her daughter, who he had absolutely no ties to, sleeping in the back seat. It wasn't the future they'd planned together.

'Thanks.' Harrison had no idea how things would turn out for him here but he'd figured he'd needed a new start. Who knew that would entail finally confronting his past? Something he realized had to happen if he was ever going to move on from Ruby Jones. Even if that meant having her back in his life whilst no longer being a part of hers.

'I'll just open the door.' Ruby hopped out of the car to unlock the apartment. It wasn't much, but it was home. A small rental with a communal pool and garden, it had everything she and Aimee needed. They were happy here. Especially with work and family living so close by. And now, Harrison. A complication she'd never expected but perhaps a reconnection that was overdue.

He seemed so desperate to talk to her, and perhaps she owed it to herself to hear him out so she could stop torturing herself about their past and why she'd got him so wrong.

When she turned around, the sight of him carrying her sleeping daughter in his arms just about stopped her heart. This was the man she'd been married to. The Harrison who bought ice cream to fix everything, and was there when she needed him. Who'd made her feel safe and loved. Not the man who'd so coldly left her to deal with her grief on her own, making her feel abandoned and unwanted. A pattern in her life she could have done without.

'Where shall I put her?' Harrison asked.

Ruby moved aside. 'Straight down the hall, first room on the left.'

As he walked into her home, Ruby couldn't help the feeling that this marked a turning point of some kind as her past and present collided. This was the home she'd created for her and Aimee once she'd finally moved out of her parents' place. A new start. Seeing Harrison in it, the reemerging feelings of admiration and something more she didn't want to acknowledge, felt like some sort of home invasion. Leaving her fearful that she would forever associate him with somewhere that used to be her safe space.

She had to blink away images of their first place together. Where she'd been the one in his arms being carried to the bedroom in very different circumstances. They'd been so young, so in love, and so naive about what they were getting into. Everything had seemed easy then. Love was the answer to everything. Until it wasn't. It hadn't been enough to save their marriage. Or their baby.

The reality, that life sometimes steamrolled right over you, had come as a shock. One she'd had to deal with on her own whilst Harrison had apparently chosen denial. She wondered if anything had changed in him over the years. Ruby had definitely become stronger, emotionally. She didn't put up with weak men who didn't deserve her or her daughter, and though that meant she was single, she didn't regret it. There was more than her heart at risk now and she certainly wouldn't invite a man into her daughter's life who could cause her the slightest pain.

Since Harrison was on his own, starting a new position, she guessed commitment still wasn't high on his list. She didn't know if that meant the fact he'd even married her made her privileged, or unfortunate. A mistake he'd eventually realized and rectified.

'She must be like her mother. Sleeps like a log.' Harrison gently placed Aimee onto her princess bed decked with a tiara-shaped headboard and sparkly covers.

He looked so out of place in here, tucking Ruby's daughter into her bed. A masculine presence in a world of pink unicorns and fluffy rainbows. Yet, at the same time, he seemed quite at home. As though this was a role he could easily have fitted. If they'd been given the chance together.

'She snores like a warthog.' Talking about her sleeping habits seemed like a very personal thing to do with a man she hardly knew anymore. A stranger now, yet someone she'd laid beside many nights.

'Just like her mother.' Harrison grinned, and for a moment they could have been that young loved-up couple. Comfortable enough with one another that he could tease her about something so personal.

'I do not snore.' A debate which had run between them for the duration of their relationship, though she'd never been accused by anyone else of the crime. She'd convinced herself he only said it to annoy her. Teasing had been their foreplay once upon a time. Winding one another up until the only way to end the argument was with a passionate kiss, with both declared the winner.

Or perhaps, being with Harrison was the only

time she'd felt safe enough to drift into a deep, deep sleep.

Aimee murmured and rolled onto her side. Ruby made sure she wasn't lying on her injured arm, dropped a kiss on her forehead and backed quietly out of the room. She closed the door carefully after Harrison made his exit too.

'She's had quite the day,' he whispered as they moved away from the bedroom.

'The ice cream did manage to take her mind off her arm. So thank you for that.'

'My pleasure.' Harrison followed her into the living area which had an open plan kitchen.

'Can I get you a drink, or something to eat?' It didn't seem polite to rush him out the door when he'd treated her and Aimee at the diner, and given them a lift home. Despite all of the red flags about having him here in her home.

He hesitated before saying, 'I wouldn't want to inconvenience you.'

Which was Harrison code for, 'I'm hungry.'

It put a smile on Ruby's face. Some things never changed. 'It's fine. Neither of us has eaten for hours. Besides, I know how cranky you get when you're hungry.'

'Do not.' He frowned, drawing up a chair to the breakfast bar.

It was tempting to keep the teasing going, but knowing where it used to lead to was sufficient for Ruby to end it there and concentrate on cooking. She had to remember the lonely nights crying herself to sleep, bereft by his absence. Not the ones where they were cuddled up in bed. Or doing more than cuddling…

If this was the one and only time they were going to be alone in her home, she was beginning to think now was the time to finally deal with the past. At least hear what he had to say, and take some time and distance to process it before she had to see him again. Better here in private than being ambushed again at work.

After breakfast though. She was hungry, and she had a feeling that she'd lose her appetite once she heard his excuses for abandoning her.

'Would you like some help?' Harrison asked as she cooked up some bacon and eggs and placed slices of bread into the toaster.

'You could get some plates for me.' She pointed towards the cupboard on the wall which housed them, thankful that he had something to do other than watch her.

It was unnerving feeling his eyes on her, wondering if he was assessing the changes in her over the years, as she had with him. If he found her lacking in some way. Regardless that he'd broken her heart, somewhere deep down inside her, it still mattered what he thought about her. Perhaps if she got the answer as to why he'd left her the way he had, she would no longer care.

She dished up breakfast and took a seat at the other side of the counter. There was a sense of anticipation in the air between them as they ate. Perhaps both considering what they would say next to one another after the small talk ran out, and they'd have to engage in a more meaningful conversation.

Once they'd finished eating, she cleared away the dishes and sat down again, her procrastination finally running out of steam. It was time for her to finally face Harrison, and whatever it was he had to say. She only hoped she could get through this without making a scene. Be it tears or anger, whichever dominated her reaction.

Ruby leaned forward, her hands clasped on the counter. 'Okay, I'm ready.'

She wasn't. All of a sudden she felt more vulnerable than she had in years. Since raising Aimee on her own, she'd steeled herself against any further hurt, determined to put all of her energy into protecting her daughter. This was opening old wounds which had been present before her precious baby was part of her existence. She didn't want the failings of the old Ruby to undermine the strong woman she was now.

Harrison's eyes opened wide. 'Ready, ready?'

Ruby nodded, swallowing the ball of anxiety suddenly rising to her throat.

He took a deep breath, at least showing that this was a difficult subject for him too. This wasn't a matter he was taking lightly and she had some admiration for that at least. He could have brushed the whole thing off as ancient history. Indeed, in some of the scenarios she'd run in her head over the years of confronting him, that was one of the reactions she'd tried to anticipate. So it wouldn't hurt just as much. Except she was realizing now that in this moment, and how she felt about the past, if Harrison had told her it was time she moved on, she would have been devastated. She didn't know if it was better or worse knowing that this seemed as important to him as it was to her.

'Where to start…' He rubbed his hands over the stubble beginning to show on his face, suddenly looking as tired and anxious as she was.

'You could tell me why you left me to grieve for our baby on my own.' It came out sharper than she'd intended, but she'd been waiting for fifteen years to say it. To get some answers.

'It's not that easy. There are many reasons why I didn't follow you to your parents' place.'

As tempting as it was to say something sarcastic and ask him to start naming them, she wanted to keep this as civil as possible and remained silent. Waiting a few minutes more for an explanation wasn't going to hurt her any more than the fifteen years of silence.

A long sigh, as though he didn't know where to begin. 'Losing the baby was tough on both of us. I know that maybe I didn't show you how much it affected me but I was devastated.'

'It was tough.' The understatement of the century.

'I wanted to be there for you. To be strong enough to hold us both up, but in the end I couldn't even manage myself. When you left to go to your parents, I had every intention of following you. But, everything caught up with me at once and I could barely even get out of bed.'

'I'm so sorry, Harrison. I had no idea.' She'd been so wrapped up in how the miscarriage had affected her, she hadn't stopped to consider what he was going through too.

'I didn't tell you. I didn't tell anyone. Thinking I just needed to get on with things. But I couldn't. Even though you were calling and begging me to come, to tell you what was wrong, I just couldn't. It was easier just to walk away. You had your parents to look after you. I would only have brought you down further.'

'But we could have been there together. Gone through it leaning on one another.' She hated to think of him suffering as much as she had, but on his own. He was right. She'd had her parents fussing over her, feeding her and making sure she was okay. Harrison wasn't close enough to his family to seek that kind of support even if his pride would have let him.

Harrison shrugged without showing any conviction in what she was saying. 'Perhaps. Though I don't think it would have made any difference. I was so lost in my own grief, the loss of our future as a family, I don't think I could have been there for you the way you needed.'

Ruby wished she'd had the chance to find out. If she'd known he'd felt anything other than relief that he wasn't tied to her forever, it could have changed everything. Even if they hadn't stayed together, it might have saved her some of the heartbreak she'd gone through. At least then she would have known it wasn't her fault. That he'd cared too. Maybe too much.

'I wish you'd tried. Or at least told me how you felt.' Finding out now wasn't doing anything to make her feel better, only worse, knowing he was grieving on his own too. That he hadn't felt secure enough in their relationship to confide in her, if no one else.

In hindsight, she supposed everyone's condolences and support had been focused on her, but Harrison had lost the baby too. He might not have carried it, or had morning sickness every day, but he'd been as much part of the pregnancy as she had. They hadn't planned the baby, but the second they'd seen the positive test, he'd started making plans. How he was going to decorate the nursery, what football team it was going to support, and he'd told her he was going to be the kind of father he wished he'd had. A present one. Not just a man who came and went and paid the bills in between.

Harrison had charted every precious day. A countdown until they became a family marked on the calendar with an *x*. They only made it a third of the way through the calendar before it had been torn down and thrown in the bin. Their dreams of a happy family over.

He'd shut down then. That was why she'd turned to her parents in search of emotional support. Travelling back to them rather than stay another moment in their home so full of reminders of everything they'd lost.

Harrison had stayed in contact at first. Always making excuses about why he couldn't follow her just yet. Phone calls soon became texts, until they'd dwindled away altogether. He'd even stopped answering her calls. It had been hard not to think she'd done something to make him realize he'd be happier on his own. How could she have known that had been a cry for help? She should have gone and seen him in person instead of wallowing in her own misery and feeling sorry for herself. Neither of them had fought hard enough to save their relationship, and failed at the first hurdle. Albeit a traumatic one.

When Harrison looked at her she could see the pain in his eyes as he relived it. They should have been there to hug and cry it all out together. Perhaps then they wouldn't still be holding on to all this pain fifteen years later.

'I just couldn't. You were already so broken and I didn't want to add to your burden. I thought I could just push on through. I was wrong.'

'So what happened?' Given the strength of his feelings, and the way he'd so desperately wanted to speak to her, Ruby suspected there was more to the story.

'I lost it for a while. Emotionally. A breakdown of sorts. It took me some time to get back on my feet. I knew you would have moved on by then and I thought a clean start was best for both of us.'

Ruby didn't know how to process what he was telling her. He was putting her through a range of emotions with every revelation. Sympathy for how alone he must have felt, anger for not including her in that decision-making process, but an overriding sense of sadness over their loss. Not only of the child they never got to meet, but of their relationship, past, present and future.

'It wasn't as easy as that for either of us.' By the sound of things, Harrison had taken his time grieving too before making some attempt at functioning. She knew how hard that was to let go and try and make a future again. One very different to the one they'd planned together.

'No, but I just wanted to explain. I'd probably do things differently now, but I was young and didn't know how to deal with all the emotions I had. It's not an excuse, but I owe it to you to tell you why I disappeared. I'm sorry.' He got up from his seat, grabbed his jacket, and moved towards the door as though the conversation was over.

It wasn't. Not by a long shot.

'Wait, Harrison. You can't go now.' Acting without thinking, she reached out and grabbed his arm. Circling her fingers around his thick, bare wrist. Skin-on-skin contact which felt as though she'd just grabbed hold of a live wire. An instant charge of electricity zapping through her body. As though one touch from Harrison had just reawakened her body from slumber. Her own Sleeping Beauty moment. Okay, so he hadn't kissed her, but that brief reconnection was enough to remind her of every kiss, every passionate, intimate moment they'd ever shared.

Ruby stared at her hand, his arm, and up at his face, to find him staring at her with equal intensity. It felt very much like she were having an out-of-body experience. On the outside looking in, trying to make sense of what was happening.

Now that he'd shared his pain with her, finally given her the answer to the question which had dogged her for fifteen years, she allowed herself to feel more than anger towards him. In hearing him out she'd given herself permission to still care, still be attracted to him and remember what they'd once had together. Except they were both very different people now, with different lives. Ones which didn't include one another.

She slowly withdrew her hand, still tingling from where she'd touched him.

'Sorry. I just wanted to say you've nothing to beat yourself up for. We can't change the past. We were young, and probably in over our heads. I wish things had been different…' It was hard not to think about how different her life would've turned out if they'd been brave and mature enough to deal with their problems the right way. They might have had a family together by now, living the life they thought they'd signed up for when they'd said their wedding vows.

'But then you wouldn't have Aimee, and I would never have denied you that.' His smile was equally as heartbreaking as his sad eyes. He was happy that she had gone on to have another child, even if it wasn't with him. Ruby wasn't sure that she would have been that understanding or generous if tables had been turned.

In fact, if he'd had a child with someone else and she'd still been on her own, it likely would have devastated her all over again. She appreciated the fact that he'd said it so she didn't feel guilty, but it also proved his more mature attitude. It seemed they'd both done a lot of growing up since their marriage ended.

'No. I suppose there's no point in looking back.' Not anymore. Their baby would never be forgotten but the loss should no longer define who they were. At least now she had her answers, closure of sorts, it might not be quite as painful when she did find herself thinking about the past.

'Looking forward, I hope we can work together without letting our history affect us too much. I mean, I know it's something we can't deny that happened, nor would I ever want to. I just—'

'You don't want things to be awkward,' she offered for him, seeing how uncomfortable he looked. It was little wonder given how she'd 'welcomed' him to the department.

Harrison was going to be around for the foreseeable future. It was something she was simply going to have to accept. Even though it was going to take some getting used to. They already had one patient in common, and there were going to be others. They couldn't avoid one another if they wanted to. At least, not forever.

'Right. So, er, where do we go from here?'

Ruby noticed now that his demeanour had changed. They were back to being virtual strangers. Polite. Distant. She wondered if that was because he'd shared so much of himself that he now felt exposed, vulnerable somehow. Or, was there a chance that because she acted like a love-struck schoolgirl when she touched him, he couldn't wait to get away?

Either way, it was probably for the best that he left now. If they had anything more to say to one another it could be done at work. Where it might not feel so personal, intimate even.

'Tell me something, Harrison. What was it you wanted to achieve with this? Forgiveness? Clearing your conscience? Then I think we've managed that. Thank you for being man enough to share all of that with me. Not everyone would have been brave enough to confront those painful memories head-on in order to move forward. You've given me what I needed too. Closure. I don't see why we can't be civil to one another at work. From now on we're simply colleagues, and I look forward to seeing you again in the future.'

She managed to restrain from holding her hand out for a handshake, though that's exactly how formal she felt saying the words. Trying to keep all emotion out of it because right now they were all mixed up in her head.

Harrison gave a curt nod of the head and simply said, 'Thanks, Ruby.'

Then he turned and walked away.

She couldn't help but wonder if this marked the end of a chapter in her life, or the beginning of a new one. Perhaps both.

CHAPTER FOUR

'HELLO, EUGENE. MY name's Dr Blake. I'm going to be performing your surgery today. I just wanted to come in and say hello.' Harrison didn't know if the child could hear him, or if he would remember the conversation. The extent of the boy's injuries were such that he had to remain sedated in ICU.

Nevertheless, Harrison liked to keep all of his patients informed of who he was and what he was going to be doing. It built up a rapport, or in this case, at least gave him a chance to see his patient before they went into the operating room. To remember Eugene was more than a name on a schedule.

He looked so small and vulnerable lying on the hospital bed hooked up to the machines monitoring his vital signs. His parents, who were still being treated for their injuries in the ICU at St Michael's Hospital in Boulder City, wouldn't be able to comfort him or walk him down to theatre. The least Harrison could do was give him five minutes of his time so he wasn't on his own.

His line of work meant he was always dealing with people at their most vulnerable, in pain, often with life-changing, or life-limiting injuries. The children were the hardest to deal with. He'd gone into the profession hoping to save lives when he hadn't been able to help his brother, or his baby. Unfortunately, that wasn't always the case. It had taken him some time to learn how to separate work from his personal feelings. At least to the extent where he didn't fall into another pit of grief.

He wondered how Ruby did it when she had a daughter she no doubt compared every young patient to. Putting herself in the parents' shoes. He supposed it was a mark of how good she was at her job that she didn't crumble either. The night of the gas explosion he'd seen for himself how motivated and efficient she was, despite upsetting circumstances.

It had been two days since he'd seen her and he'd been glad of a little space. Unburdening himself of the guilt and grief of that time fifteen years ago had come at a price. It had left a mark in sharing so much personal information with Ruby. Making him question if he'd done the right thing, and if she'd think badly of him.

Although she'd seemed to understand, there was still part of him that thought he should have been able to 'man up' at the time. That a stronger man would have been able to suck up those feelings of loss and simply get on with life instead of letting them overwhelm him. In opening up to Ruby, those questions had resurfaced again. Perhaps it would have been better to simply let things lie. Not to have interacted with Ruby in a personal manner at all.

Especially when they seemed to have fallen so easily into companionship, eating and chatting together as if they hadn't undergone the trauma of losing their baby and been separated all this time. Even though finding out about Aimee's existence had come as something of a shock, she had taken to him too. In their time at the diner they could have been viewed as any other family. Except Ruby was no longer his wife, and her daughter wasn't his.

Perhaps in a parallel universe another Harrison had coped better with his grief and he had that happy family, but not in this one. Not ever. Because he couldn't afford to open his heart again to anyone, much less a child. He'd had one chance to be a father and fate had decided otherwise. As far as he was concerned that was a sign. It wasn't meant to be, and he'd accepted that because, as he'd discovered, the alternative had the possibility of being too painful to even contemplate.

Harrison was about to leave to see his day patients when Ruby walked into the room. Despite knowing they were working in the same hospital, and there was always a possibility of running into her, his pulse picked up at the sight of her. He supposed it was due to years without a glimpse of the only woman he'd ever loved. Although that didn't explain why his body felt like it had been hit by lightning when she'd grabbed his arm in her kitchen. It seemed time and distance hadn't managed to tame that spark she set off inside him with a simple touch.

Their chemistry had always been off the charts. However, they weren't horny, loved-up teenagers anymore. They were divorced virtual strangers now, and he'd have to work reminding himself of that.

'I thought I'd check in on our patient,' she said, approaching Eugene's bedside.

'He's stable, at least. I'll be taking him to the OR later this afternoon to debride the burns. Then I'll be able to see if he's going to need further surgery.' Harrison was hoping Eugene wouldn't need skin grafts as it would be a long recovery process, but at least his young skin would hopefully stretch and lessen the chances of painful contracting as he grew.

'Bless him." She gestured for Harrison to step away from the bed obviously wanting to discuss something away from the boy. "I hear his parents are in a bad way too.' It was clear the family had been on Ruby's mind too. He should have known her interest in her patients wouldn't stop once they were moved from her department. She'd always been a nurturing figure. Even in school, whenever one of the younger children fell or hurt themselves, it was Ruby they went to for words of comfort before being patched up by the school nurse. She'd been born to be a nurse, and a mother. He was glad she'd achieved both. She'd done better for herself once he'd gone from her life.

'They are, but hopefully they will all recover. Even if it takes some time.' Not everyone's body reacted to burns the same way. There could be unforeseen complications that didn't immediately present, but that was where the burns specialists came in. Harrison knew the staff at St Michael's and they would perform whatever surgery was necessary in the future. For now, it was important to keep them stable in the intensive care unit.

It was difficult to see an entire family suffer in such circumstances but he hoped they would help pull one another through. He hated to think that young Eugene could be orphaned, or that his parents might never see him grow up. From personal experience, he knew how traumatic that was, and they'd all been through enough already.

'Will you keep me updated?' Ruby asked, tucking the covers around Eugene's small form on the bed, her mothering instinct taking over. At least he would have someone to look over him even though his parents couldn't be here.

'I will. We haven't been able to track down any other family, so he'll be here on his own for some time.' Although there would be staff coming and going on the ward, it was a shame the boy wouldn't have anyone to come and sit with him, talk to him and make sure he wasn't on his own. Even though he wasn't conscious, there was always that chance that he'd be able to hear anything going on around him. He'd experienced major trauma and hospitals were frightening places at the best of times for children. A reassuring voice could make all the difference.

'I'll try and stop by when I can. I could bring some of Aimee's books to read to him.' It was clear the little boy had touched Ruby, as much as he had Harrison. Perhaps it was their shared experience of losing a child themselves which made them more empathetic with his plight, or they were simply two medical professionals who saw their positions as more than just a job.

Either way, Harrison knew they weren't going to let this boy lie here without visitors for the duration of his stay.

'I'm sure his parents would appreciate that. How is Aimee doing by the way?' They'd both been on his mind since that day. More so than he would have hoped.

'She's good. Thinks she should have ice cream for breakfast every morning, but other than that she's recovering well.' Ruby narrowed her eyes at him so he knew he was responsible for that situation, but it wasn't long before she was smiling at him again. The quick change made his pulse flutter again.

Something about that look made him remember when they'd been together, and teasing had simply been part of their relationship dynamic. Keeping things fun between them. He was glad to see that she was still young at heart and not so changed despite the years and her important role in work and at home.

'Sorry, but I'm glad there are no long-lasting effects.' Harrison did his best to look sheepish so she would forgive him. Whilst he was used to being the fun doctor cheering up his young patients, he had no experience in parenting. Something he was reminded of when he'd seen Ruby and Aimee together. A sight which would forever cause a pang in his heart for what should have been.

'She keeps asking after you actually. You definitely made a fan.' Whilst Ruby didn't appear overly enthused by the development, Harrison was glad he'd made a good impression on one new acquaintance. And okay, it didn't hurt that she might put in a good word for him with her mother.

'And she has one in me. Aimee is a credit to you.' Now that they'd had a real heart-to-heart, he hoped Ruby would thaw towards him too. Even though they would never have the same relationship they'd once had, she'd always been a big part of his life. Including those years apart. Just because she wasn't present in his everyday existence, it didn't mean he didn't think about her, or their baby. She was always there in the back of his mind, affecting his every decision.

He suspected that was what had even spurred him to finish his medical studies. Knowing that one day they might cross paths, and wanting her to be proud of him. Not always hating him, and believing that he was a poor excuse for a man. Hopefully now she understood that whilst he was probably too emotionally immature to deal with the tragedy at the time, their separation had been about more than she could ever have imagined.

Yet, he hadn't been able to find the words to tell her about his brother. Why the miscarriage had triggered such a catastrophic reaction in him. Therapy had helped him work through a lot of his issues, but talking about Joey was still painful. It was a subject which seemed a step too far to broach when they'd just met again after such a long time.

Perhaps he'd never have the opportunity, or motivation to share that most personal information. Certainly, it wasn't something he'd discussed with any other colleague, friend or lover. There was no reason to expect that Ruby would be anything more than a work acquaintance now. Only time would tell if they found it too difficult to be around one another, or if their bond was something they'd welcome back into their lives.

On his part, he'd missed Ruby. His reasons for not contacting her obvious in the circumstances. But now that they were on speaking terms again, he realized what he'd thrown away fifteen years ago.

Apart from being the love of his life, Ruby had been his best friend, his confidante and the only person who'd really made him feel loved since his brother had died.

And as far as she'd been aware at the time, he'd simply walked away from her as if none of it had meant anything to him. Never knowing it was thoughts of her which had kept him going in the darkest times. Telling himself that one day he would be well enough, free of his grief, to find her and tell her how sorry he was.

Except that had been a longer journey than he'd ever expected, and even when he was functioning again, he was too fragile, too afraid to make contact. Unable to take that step in case she rejected him. Instead, leaving the way open for her to move on even if he couldn't, by filing for divorce.

He was glad she had, and though she didn't owe him anything, he hoped he could have her in his life again in some capacity. But he wasn't going to push her too hard to make that happen when she'd been through so much, and had a lot to process after everything he'd shared with her so far.

He'd waited this long to see her again and he was sure it couldn't hurt any more to wait a little longer.

'I guess I should get back to work.' As much as he wanted to stay and spend time with Ruby, he was still new here, and he wanted to make a good impression on the rest of the medical staff as well as his patients.

'Me too.' Ruby moved away from Eugene's bedside as well, giving him one last lingering look as if trying to leave a part of her to comfort the boy.

'I'm sure I'll see you around.' Harrison found himself reluctant to make that final break away from her, not knowing when he would see her again, or if they would even get another chance to talk.

'I'm sure you will.' She gave him a little smile, offering some hope.

If they hadn't had a complicated, tragic history, and they were two single people who'd just met, he might have seen this as an opportunity to ask for a date. As it was, he was lucky she was even talking to him. Still, she was leaving the door open for a future meet and that was enough for now.

They were making their way towards the door when the alarms sounded from the patient's cubicle opposite Eugene's. Both Harrison and Ruby immediately turned back, knowing someone's life was in jeopardy. The monitors were already showing a sharp decline in the young woman's vital signs.

'Her blood pressure is dangerously low,' Harrison noted aloud.

'She came into the ER a few nights ago. Lucille, I think her name was. She'd had a miscarriage, but some of the placenta had remained. The last I'd seen of her was when she'd been wheeled down to theatre for surgery.' Thankfully Ruby was able to give him a quick patient history to save some time. This wasn't the area Harrison specialized in, but he'd had some training in obstetrics during his placement.

Although the nurses would be on their way once they'd heard the monitors scream their warning, he hit the emergency button on the wall to call for extra help.

'It could be septic shock if infection has set in. Her skin is clammy and her heart rate and breathing is rapid.'

Except now the heart monitor was flatlining, indicating that the patient was in cardiac arrest. They needed to get her heart pumping blood around her body before they did anything else.

'Her lips are turning blue. I'm going to see where the resus team are.' Ruby rushed off, returning only moments later with the defibrillator and a team of nurses.

Between them, Harrison and Ruby attached the sticky pads to Lucille's chest, which would conduct the charge from the defibrillator to her heart, and hopefully restart it.

He let Ruby take over, figuring she would have more experience in this area since she worked in the emergency room.

'Stand clear,' she issued to the assembled staff once the defibrillator was charged, then delivered the first shock in the hope of restarting Lucille's heart.

Harrison checked the woman's vital signs. 'Nothing.'

'We go again. Charging. Stand clear.' A focused Ruby watched and waited before delivering another shock.

'Checking for shockable rhythm,' Harrison announced as per protocol, letting everyone know what was happening step by step.

Thankfully, the blip on the screen and the gradual colour returning to the woman's lips let them both breathe a momentary sigh of relief.

'We've got her,' he confirmed, then there was a flurry of activity whilst they did their best to stabilize the patient.

'Sorry if we stepped on anyone's shoes,' Ruby said tongue-in-cheek to the attending physicians now present. As aware as Harrison was that this wasn't their department. They just happened to be in the right place at the right time.

'No problem. We're glad you were here. Thanks.' The senior medic for the department came forward as they stood back.

Once Harrison gave them a rundown of what had happened, and what they suspected, he was happy to let them take over. He and Ruby had done their bit, and now it would be down to the surgical team to treat her.

As he made his exit with Ruby, the adrenaline rush wearing off, he was beginning to feel that familiar jittery energy which accompanied an unexpected medical emergency. The sort of post-trauma effect that needed to be processed before normality resumed. It said a lot about Ruby's strength of character when she did this every shift.

He stopped in the corridor just ahead of her, making her come to a standstill too. 'Are you okay?'

'Yes. Of course. I'm just glad we got her back.' Her eyes were too bright, her smile too broad, for him to believe. Although they'd been apart for years he still knew her, and this was Ruby putting on a brave face.

Apart from the near-death experience of the patient, there was the miscarriage aspect. A baby had died, along with whatever dreams of the future the young mother had harboured. Something too close to home to be ignored. It was playing on Harrison's mind, bringing back memories and emotions of when Ruby had lost their baby. A sharp stab to the heart with every recollection.

The baby books they'd read, marking the size of their little jelly bean with every passing week. Tiny bootees and cardigans Ruby had knitted in neutral colours for their son or daughter. Then there was the crib Harrison had been carefully building himself. A surprise for Ruby, which he'd smashed to pieces in the end without her ever seeing the labour of love he'd created. Too painful a reminder to have kept. Redundant along with everything else they'd been putting aside for their baby, except their love. That was one thing which had never been packed away in the hope of forgetting it had ever existed. He'd lived with that hole in his heart where his baby should have been, every day of his life since. Seeing someone else go through that pain and loss wasn't easy to watch. Yet he hadn't been the one carrying their baby. His body hadn't changed, nor had it struggled to adapt when the pregnancy ended much too soon. Ruby had gone through so much physically as well as emotionally, it seemed selfish that he'd been the one to run away and leave her to deal with everything on her own.

In his defence, he'd known her parents were looking after her better than he could, given the emotional state he'd been in too, but still, he hated that he'd left her side. Up until then, they'd done everything together, and he'd left her when she'd needed him most. When he'd needed her most. Who knew, if he'd been able to think clearer at the time, been able to express his feelings too, they might have been able to pull each other through the dark times. They might have saved their relationship, even gone on to have that family together. It was an even greater tragedy that he'd never know for sure.

'Are you okay?' Ruby was staring at him intently like she might have already asked the question and he hadn't heard her, so lost in thoughts of the past.

There was no way she'd come out of this scenario unscathed.

'I'm good. I was just thinking we should probably find the time to try and de-stress at the end of the day. In the circumstances, I don't think it's good that we keep everything in, and no one else would understand better than we do. I don't have anyone else to talk to.' Harrison realized as he was talking, as much as he was concerned about Ruby's well-being, that his mattered too.

He'd learned not to bottle things up, it wasn't good for anyone's mental health. As he was new in town, he had no one else to talk to. Despite not wanting to burden her with any more of his personal issues, it might be good for them to have one another's backs.

'What are you suggesting? A drink?' She watched him with suspicious eyes and he couldn't blame her. He'd already proved spectacularly that she couldn't trust him. But, on this occasion, he intended to be there for her.

'A drink sounds great. Point me to the nearest dive bar and we'll decompress once we're done.' He'd actually just intended a coffee or something, but since she'd brought up the idea, he wouldn't mind having a drink somewhere with Ruby. It would almost be like old times. Apart from the fact they were divorced, and they weren't likely to be ID'd these days.

'Hmm… I suppose we could probably both do with one. Give me your number. It's not like I have anyone else to talk to about work, or anything else to do. I should be finished by eight, but I'll nip home to sort Aimee out. I'm sure my parents won't mind babysitting if they think I'm going out for the night. On second thoughts, maybe I shouldn't tell them I'm meeting their ex-son-in-law. I'm not sure they've forgiven you yet.'

Harrison flinched, though it was a well-deserved blow. It was little wonder that they should still hold a grudge when he'd left Ruby's parents to pick up the pieces and stick her back together again. He didn't suppose any excuse would ever appease them when he'd hurt their precious daughter so badly.

'Hopefully in time…'

Ruby raised her eyebrows suggesting hell might well freeze over before that happened.

'You could put in a good word for me, and I know I've got Aimee onside.' He hoped he wouldn't be the devil incarnate forever.

'It'll take time, Harrison.'

Forgiveness wasn't something which could be rushed and he understood that. He was just glad he and Ruby were on better terms than he probably deserved.

Harrison texted her so she had his number.

'I'm willing to wait.' He'd been on good terms with her parents until everything had become too much for him. They'd accepted him into their family and no doubt his disappearance had felt like a betrayal to them too. What no one knew, or could possibly understand, was how that separation had been devastating to him too. Losing everyone he'd ever been close to and suddenly finding himself alone, in despair, and not knowing where to turn. He'd spent some time with his mother, but they hadn't been close since Joey's death, and burdening her with his grief over the loss of his child had felt unfair. She'd almost seemed relieved when he'd moved on, seeking help from the medical profession instead of those he was supposed to be closest to.

'That makes a change,' she said, a mischievous twinkle in her eyes, letting him know that she hadn't completely forgiven and forgotten either. He still had a lot to make up to her, but he was willing to do it. His conscience demanded it, along with the new dynamic developing between them, which he was keen to explore a little more.

'Ouch.' He clutched his chest theatrically, making her smile. 'I guess I deserve that, but I promise I intend to do everything in my power to try and make amends.'

There was nothing he could do that would ever wipe out that mistake, but that just meant he'd be trying for a long time. Until Ruby got fed up with him, or got used to having him around.

'Drinks are on you, then, Dr Blake.'

'If you're lucky I might even treat you to some chips and dip.'

'Don't go spoiling me, I'm not used to it.' A laughing Ruby handed his phone back to him before walking away, looking and sounding lighter than she had since they'd become reacquainted.

This was the Ruby he remembered. Not the broken one he'd left, unable to bear seeing her in so much pain when he couldn't make things better for her—or for himself. Though he didn't know that if given that time over again he could do things any differently. To change the outcome of their relationship would have meant opening up to Ruby completely about the loss of his brother. A grief he still found too difficult to confront and he needed to avoid it, and Ruby, to ensure he didn't slip back into that darkness.

Although he had this deep need for her forgiveness, and their paths were inevitably going to cross at work, he had to keep himself protected. Just as he had all those years ago.

CHAPTER FIVE

'WHERE ARE YOU GOING, Mommy?' A sleepy Aimee curled up on Ruby's lap, burying her head in her mother's chest and making her feel guilty about leaving her again.

'I'm just meeting a friend. I won't be long, and Grandma is going to tuck you into bed.' Ruby gave her mother the nod to extract her clinging child and put her to bed. She still had to change before she joined Harrison for that much-needed drink. Though she had an inkling this was about more than winding down after a difficult day.

Harrison was likely wanting time to process what had happened with Lucille too. It was never easy dealing with the loss of someone else's baby at work. Trying to put personal feelings aside to concentrate on those of the patient, and treating her the way Ruby wished she had been treated. With sympathy and understanding.

Something which had been missing with some of the medical staff when she'd miscarried, because of her age. Many assuming 'it was better for her,' that she could always have more children when she was ready. Assuming that hers hadn't been a cherished, highly anticipated baby simply because it had been an unplanned pregnancy. It was still the loss of a precious child no matter what the circumstances, and nothing could ever hope to replace it. Even having Aimee hadn't filled that void inside her. It had given her renewed purpose, someone else to love, but as far as Ruby was concerned, she was a mother to two babies.

Perhaps the cavalier attitude from some towards her loss at the time had been what had spurred her on to finish her medical studies once she'd worked through her grief. So she could provide better treatment, more empathy, to young women just like her. She was glad she'd been able to do that for so many patients in the emergency room over the years, and it went some way to easing the hurt. Even if cases like Lucille's were difficult to deal with objectively.

Ruby brushed the hair from Aimee's face as her mother tucked her into her bed. 'Goodnight, sweet girl.'

She dropped a kiss on the forehead of her

now sleeping daughter, before exiting the room with her mother.

'It's Harrison isn't it?' her mother said, arms folded, lips pursed, as soon as the door was closed behind them.

Ruby sighed. There was no point in denying it when she had nothing to hide. 'Yes. It's just a drink. We have a lot to talk over.'

Her mother didn't know they'd already had their heart-to-heart, or the very personal information he'd shared with her. It was private. Just like what had happened with them at work today. Some things they could only share with one another. She was telling herself that was the only reason she'd agreed to this drink.

A tut from her mother in response. 'I won't say anything to your father, because I don't want to send his blood pressure soaring but please be careful. I know you have a tendency to lose all common sense around this boy. Don't forget the state Harrison Blake left you in the last time you were together.'

Her mother's concern made her smile when it hadn't changed over the years. As far as she was concerned, Ruby was still her baby girl and she would go 'mama bear on the rampage' to protect her. Ruby suspected she would be equally as protective over her own cub.

'He's not a boy, Mom. He's a grown man, and

I'm a grown woman. We're not together, but we do have a history I can't ignore. I'm well aware of how much he hurt me before, and you and Dad were the ones left to pick up the pieces, but this is just a drink between colleagues. Nothing more.' Ruby kissed her mother on the cheek, trying to convince her as much as herself that there was no need to read anything more into this.

Even though she proceeded to spread the contents of her closet all over her bed before settling on an outfit she thought looked good without conveying how much effort she'd gone to for simple drinks with a colleague.

Since Harrison was new in town, Ruby had decided to show him some of the tourist sights on the main strip. She met him by the fountains, just as they began their nightly light show, the water dancing in time to music and putting on quite the display.

He smiled when he spotted her walking towards him and she was powerless against the little flip her heart gave at the sight of him. One of the new attractions standing there in his well-worn dark denims and blue-and-white-checked shirt. He was leaning casually against a billboard, thumbs hooked in the waistband of his jeans as though he was waiting to be picked up. It gave Ruby a secret thrill that it was her he was waiting for, and seemed to be oblivious to the admiring glances from passers-by, when he was so focused on her approach.

Time and heartache apparently hadn't lessened the impact he still had on her. Her mother's words rang in her ears, reminding her that she had to keep her head. Not get caught up in romantic fantasies when their reality had been far from perfect.

'Hey,' she said when she was finally standing in front of him. Butterflies taking flight in her tummy when he kissed her on the cheek.

'Hey. You look lovely, Ruby.'

'Thanks.' It was ridiculous that she was feeling so nervous when they'd clarified that this wasn't a date. He was her ex-husband for a reason. Obviously, lack of physical attraction hadn't been part of that decision. As long as she kept hold of the emotionally closed-off part of him which had left her curled up in the foetal position, crying and alone, there shouldn't be a problem.

Apart from the fact he'd already opened up to her more over the course of these past few days than he had for the duration of their marriage…

'So, I'm at your mercy tonight. Where are we going for that drink? I don't see many dark quiet bars around here where we can hide away from the milling crowds.' He glanced around at the throng of locals and tourists all out seeing the sights and sampling everything that Las Vegas had to offer, seeming almost overwhelmed.

It had that effect at first. The bright neon flashing lights, the loud music, and the smell from food vendors all conspired to overload the senses when first encountered. She didn't notice it anymore. Not that she ventured here at night very often. In fact, she couldn't even remember the last time she'd been out on a date. Meeting an actual man who wasn't a patient or a colleague, who simply wanted to take her out for the evening.

Relationships since Harrison hadn't exactly been successful, and she included Aimee's father in that group. Perhaps it was because she was already juggling work and motherhood, the most important things in her life, leaving no room for anyone else. There was also the possibility that she'd never loved anyone the way she'd loved Harrison, and since that hadn't worked out, she'd lost all hope of finding someone she would spend the rest of her life with. Still, it was nice to be out in any capacity, free from her usual responsibilities.

'You'd be surprised.' She pulled a bag of quarters from her purse and shook them at him.

'Gambling? Really? You've changed, Ruby Jones.'

'More than you will ever know,' she muttered, leading him to the dark side with her.

The intimidating security staff outside the casino nodded at them as they made their way up the steps to the entrance, flashing yellow lights directing them inside. Ruby strutted in through the marble hallway as though this were an everyday occurrence, when in reality she'd never set foot in this place. She'd heard a few of the nurses talking about this place with the sexy little bar in the back but never had the chance to check it out for herself.

'Wow. This place is a real assault on the senses, isn't it?' Harrison spun around, taking in the high ceilings and the armless statues, the noise of the whirring slot machines almost drowning him out.

'You ain't seen nothing yet.' Ruby grinned, taking him by the hand and leading him farther into the den of iniquity.

The main gaming floor was a hive of activity and sound. The buzz of the machines, clatter of coins and the happy cheers of winners gave it a carnival atmosphere. They walked the psychedelic carpet past the entranced zombie-like players feeding machines with their hard-earned cash, towards the dimly lit bar in the back. In stark contrast to the gamblers' paradise with its moody lighting and reserved clientele, it was an antidote to the madness outside.

'Well, this is a change of pace,' Harrison noted as they selected a booth to sit in.

'It's early. There's usually a show on later.' Ruby didn't anticipate they'd still be here at that time and had no idea if there would be a band playing, or a burlesque show provided as entertainment. It was hard to tell when the aged red leather seats and fringed table lamps alluded to either. For now, however, it provided the privacy and quiet Harrison might want to enable a conversation. As well as the alcohol he'd promised to get her through it.

'Very salubrious,' he said with a grin, pressing the brass button on the wall of the booth, which apparently provided table service.

A few minutes later, a broad-shouldered barman wearing a muscle-enhancing, too-tight black T-shirt appeared with a pad and pencil to take their order. It didn't seem the time or place to order cocktails, her usual go-to drink on the rare occasion she did go out, so she ordered a beer along with Harrison.

'I thought we could have our post-work analysis here, then we can use gambling to distract us from our emotional issues.' She was joking, though she would never have brought Harrison here if she thought there was any chance of him having a real problem with gambling.

He'd always been very careful with money. Saving every cent in order to give them both a better life. She doubted he'd changed that much over the years that he'd developed any sort of addiction. Harrison Blake had always been a very careful man and she'd loved that about him. Believing that he was safe, would always take care of her and never let her down. She'd been wrong then, but tonight was about trying to put that behind them and have a little fun.

'Dark. Very dark, Nurse Jones.' He shook his head, but the grin remained in place.

A dry sense of humour was needed in their profession to get them through difficult working days. They both knew gambling, like any other addiction, was a serious matter. She'd dealt with the aftermath of many huge losses in places like this. Depression often lead to more serious health problems when people lost jobs and relationships over their addiction. Las Vegas had more than its fair share of people for whom gambling was more than a bit of fun, and as a result, they'd seen those who'd hit rock bottom in the emergency room.

On this occasion, however, she was hoping a flutter in the casino would detract somewhat from the chat she knew they were about to have.

'So, today was a doozy, wasn't it?' She took a sip of beer from one of the bottles their waiter set down in front of them.

'You could say that. Is the hospital always this eventful?' Harrison asked, tracing the drops of condensation on his beer bottle with his thumb.

Ruby wondered if he was regretting his move already. The thought pained her more than it should. She was just getting used to having him around again. The idea that he wasn't happy, or worse, that he might move away again, would be hard to bear.

'I know Boulder City isn't too far away, but this is more of a tourist destination for people to enjoy all of life's excesses and we're probably busier than you're used to at St Michael's. In saying that, you've met with more challenges in a couple of days than I would usually experience in a week.' She offered him a smile, hoping she could persuade him it wasn't such a bad place to be.

Given their history, she should have been glad if he was having second thoughts about his new position. It would make life easier for her if he disappeared back out of her life. Not that it guaranteed that he would be gone from her thoughts. Fifteen years had proved that to her.

However, this time they were spending together was helping to heal some old wounds. Working through issues they should have discussed back then might just help them both finally move on from their tragedy.

'That's something, I guess.' He looked downcast, picking off the beer label with his thumbnail, clearly thinking about something that made him sad.

Ruby refrained from asking him what it was, waiting until he was ready to tell her.

'How do you help someone like Lucille without completely breaking down?' The question, combined with the anguish in his eyes when he glanced up at her, tugged unexpectedly on her heartstrings. It never occurred to her that dealing with the patient today would have triggered him, or that he might have been thinking about her during that frantic time.

Seeing his genuine pain stole away the bravado she would otherwise have tried to portray so he wouldn't see how affected she could still be. There didn't seem any point when he was clearly still hurting as much as she was over their loss.

Another swig of alcohol strengthened her resolve before she spoke on the matter.

'How do you know I don't?' She was only half teasing, there were times she did break down in the privacy of her own home after dealing with such cases, but she made it sound like a joke. Managing to tug his mouth into a half-smile.

'Because I saw you in action today. Calm, professional and compassionate. Knowing what you went through, and how you handled it, I'm in awe.'

'You did the same. We were both out of our comfort zone there today, but we did our bit to save Lucille all the same.' Ruby was uneasy accepting any praise for simply doing her job. As always, in putting the patient first, it was important that she did put her personal feelings aside. At least until she was no longer in the workplace.

'I'm aware of that. I have to say, though, my area of expertise means I'm not confronted too often with such stark memories of the past. It is something however, I feel you are faced with relatively frequently.'

Ruby shrugged. 'It's all part of the job. Yes, it hurts, Harrison. Is that what you want me to say? It will never not hurt. We lost our baby. It was traumatic and it's something I'll never get over, but I've had to learn to simply push through the grief. I can't let it affect me forever or else I couldn't do my job. I can see that you found it…challenging today, but I wouldn't have known if you hadn't told me. We worked together to save the patient, and that's what it's all about.'

It was heartening to know that Harrison wasn't the cold fish she'd taken him for when he left her, but she didn't want him to suffer forever either. And he was clearly hurting today.

He raised his bottle to her. 'Thanks for this.'

'The beer? I thought you were paying.' Ruby was deliberately obtuse, trying to keep things light. She understood why today had affected him so much. When Lucille had first come into the ER after her miscarriage, Ruby's heart had gone out to her, as it did with everyone who had gone through the same ordeal.

'The chat. I've learned not to keep everything bottled up inside, but that's not easy when you're the new guy in town. Or you've never told anyone else in your life that your child died.' After everything he'd told her, it didn't surprise Ruby that he'd never discussed his loss. She just felt sad for him that he'd never been able to confide in anyone.

'I guess no one except us understands.' Though she wasn't sure Harrison knew exactly what she'd gone through when he left, compounding her grief and loss. Just as she would never fully grasp what he'd felt at the time to think leaving her was the only option left.

'Well, thanks again for agreeing to this. I know it isn't easy for you either.'

'No, but you're right. It's better to talk things out.' She was as guilty as Harrison of not being able to open up about the past. When she'd discovered she was pregnant with Aimee there had been no discussion with the father, other than *I'm keeping the baby*. Without ever telling him about her previous pregnancy. It might not have changed the outcome, but if she'd been honest with her feelings, then perhaps they might have parted on better terms.

'Something I learned too late to save us.' Harrison gave her a look which sent the heat rising in her body.

Was it her imagination, or wishful thinking on her part, that there was more than a hint of regret in his words? Along with a flare of something in his eyes she was afraid to recognize. They'd always had great chemistry, it was communication which had let them down. Now that they were talking about their feelings, it was beginning to feel dangerous. As though the obstacles that had kept them apart were suddenly being eroded. Except she couldn't get over the fact he'd left her. Abandoned her with her grief and, though she was doing her best to forgive him, she would never forget. She couldn't, because letting him get close left her open to the same thing happening again.

And right here, right now, with Harrison looking at her so intensely, it would be easy to believe he would never hurt her. That there was a chance they could pick up where they'd left off. Especially when this was feeling more and more like a date. Something she needed to bust out of for her own sanity.

'If you're finished, why don't we go and try our luck outside?' She drained her bottle, keen to get away from the intimacy of the booth, the conversation and the company. A little distance to recompose herself.

'Sure.' Harrison sat back, that intimate connection broken, and finished his beer.

Ruby was already on her feet, waiting impatiently as he tossed a few dollars on the table, before he followed her out of the bar.

The blast of noise and light almost a relief, bringing her back down to earth and reminding her it wasn't just her and Harrison who existed.

'You'll have to take the lead. I'm a bit out of my depth on this one.' Bells ringing, and electronic screens presenting all matter of exciting opportunities to get rich quick surrounded them. A surreal experience on top of the moment he'd just had with Ruby.

Their connection, despite their years of separation, seemed as strong as ever. Which was exactly why they needed to be around other people. There was a danger of becoming too insular when they had shared experiences, and while he was open to talking these days, he wasn't ready to open up to anything more.

It was difficult. He wanted to be with Ruby because she was easy to be around. They knew each other, and had so much in common already that there was no awkwardness. At least now that they'd addressed the past and he'd acknowledged his own failings.

However, there was a danger of becoming too comfortable with her. Forgetting the reasons he'd had for walking out on their marriage in the first place. That overwhelming sense of loss he hadn't been able to properly cope with. Yes, he'd eventually been able to move on, but that hadn't removed the issue completely from his life. He'd simply taken steps to ensure he never found himself in that position again.

Safe sex, casual relationships and avoiding loving anyone the way he'd loved Ruby. That was what made his current situation so dangerous. Now that she was back in his life he had to find a different way to protect himself when they were already close. He had to find some way to keep some emotional distance, but he supposed quiet drinks and deeply personal conversations probably weren't the way to do that. Still, he'd needed to talk about what had happened today for his sake as well as Ruby's. Once they had their bit of fun in the casino they could go their separate ways again and he would try to keep their interactions limited to work.

'This isn't something I do regularly either. Maybe we should stick to the good ol' one-armed bandits.' Ruby handed him some quarters and they made their way over to a bank of brightly lit retro slot machines.

Harrison dropped a quarter in the slot, watched the wheels whir around with a sense of anticipation, before disappointment set in when he didn't win. He could see why the highs and lows of gambling became addictive. It wasn't long before he was one of those zombies going through the motions, hoping for a change in fortune. And when three red sevens lined up in the window, bells ringing, money pumping out into the tray, the euphoria was unexpected. It was barely enough to cover the cost of their two beers, yet he was pumping the air with his fist as though he'd won a million dollars.

Ruby was laughing next to him and caught up in the moment, he grabbed her into a hug and spun her around. Having her warm body back in his arms, seeing her smile, made him yearn for what they used to have. He reluctantly set her back down on her feet.

'Sorry. I got carried away,' he said, putting some distance between them again.

'That's okay,' she said, a little breathless. 'I'm just glad to see you cutting loose a little.'

'Excuse me? You think I'm not fun? Didn't we have ice cream for breakfast not so long ago?' It wounded him to think that Ruby thought he'd lost his fun side.

'Oh, yeah. You're such a rebel.' She rolled her eyes but he saw the twitch of her mouth as she teased him.

It made Harrison determined to prove to her that he was still young at heart.

He spotted a huge machine in the middle of the floor with 'Mystery Prize' spelled out in flashing LED red and amber lights atop. At a dollar per spin, it took him some time to load his previous winnings. He had no clue what he was doing but he did know that this was the first time he'd felt alive in a long time.

Having Ruby by his side, trying to impress her with his spontaneous side reminded him of when they'd been teenagers and he'd been showing off on the football field, trying to get her attention. Despite a spectacular fall, and the team's ultimate defeat, he'd had his wish granted. Ruby had spent the rest of the evening treating his cuts and bruises, giving him plenty of time to charm her. Although they were never going to be those love-struck teens again, that need to impress her was apparently alive and well.

He pulled the lever using two hands and watched the reels spin with bated breath. To no avail.

'Your turn,' he said, stepping back to let Ruby try her luck.

'Are you sure?'

'You might be luckier than I have been.' Whatever the outcome, at least he knew he'd taken a risk. Something he didn't do very often, and he had to ignore the warning bells going off in his head that Ruby should be the one making him break his own rules already.

'Fingers crossed.' She pulled the lever and stepped back, clinging onto Harrison's arm. The adrenaline rushing through his body on two counts.

Harrison held his breath, the buzz of anticipation crackling between him and Ruby.

The first reel came to a standstill, registering the 'Mystery Prize' symbol. Then the second spun around. Ruby's grasp on his arm became tighter as they fixated their gaze on that last reel. It seemed to take forever before it stopped, landing the much anticipated third 'Mystery Prize' icon. In the split second it took Harrison to realise they'd hit the jackpot, bells were ringing, sirens blaring and lights flashing. Announcing the win to everyone in the vicinity. A shower of gold confetti landed around them to confirm their win.

'Congratulations!' A smart-looking man in a black suit strode up to them with a gold envelope in hand. The badge on his lapel naming him as 'Gino,' the floor manager.

'Thanks.' Harrison was a little shell-shocked as he handed over the prize to him. 'What is it?'

'A VIP night in Las Vegas for two, courtesy of Jackpot Casino, redeemable for twenty-eight days,' Gino informed them, turning them to face a camera which had suddenly appeared in front of them. Capturing their open-mouthed shock forever.

Once Gino had delivered the news and posed for the photograph, he seemed as keen to disappear as quickly as he'd arrived.

'What do we do now?' Harrison asked, his big win suddenly feeling very anticlimactic. It certainly wasn't a life-changing prize. He suspected it was something for the tourist clientele rather than a Las Vegas resident.

'Give your details at the reception desk. Congratulations again.' With that, Gino disappeared into the crowd which had gathered around them.

He smiled awkwardly at the people who'd assembled to witness his win, until they gradually lost interest and returned to increase their own chances of a life-changing win.

'Can I see?' Ruby took the envelope from him and removed the contents.

'It says you have a limo for the evening, champagne dinner and a night in the penthouse. Sounds good to me.' She enthused about the details of the prize, perhaps sensing his mild disappointment.

'It's just as well because you'll be sharing it with me.'

Ruby's eyes widened. 'What? No. Why?'

'Apart from the fact you're the only person I know in town, you pulled the lever. This is your win as much as it is mine.' It seemed only fair to share the prize with her. He reckoned she could probably do with a treat when her time was taken up with work and motherhood.

'I don't know, Harrison—' Before Ruby could turn down the offer, there was a loud commotion behind them. A crash and a scream which couldn't be ignored.

When he turned towards the source of the noise, he saw a heavy-set woman lying on the ground, a stool overturned and a pool of blood gradually spreading across the garish carpet.

Harrison and Ruby rushed over to offer their

assistance, just as a concerned-looking Gino appeared on the scene too. He radioed through for an ambulance and requested a first aid kit in the meantime.

'I'm a doctor and this is Ruby, a nurse. Can we help?' Harrison offered their assistance until the paramedics arrived.

'Yes, please. I think she bumped her head on the way down.' Gino was hovering nervously as Harrison and Ruby knelt down beside the lady on the ground. She was beginning to come around and struggling to sit up.

'You've had a fall. It's better if you stay where you are until the paramedics get here to check you over. My name is Ruby. I'm a nurse. What's your name?' Ruby was holding the woman's hand and talking to her very calmly so as not to freak her out. She'd always been good in a crisis. Perhaps that was partly why he hadn't been able to cope with the aftermath of the miscarriage. It had been too hard to see her broken like that, knowing he was powerless to do anything about it.

'Moira,' the woman said, clearly a little disoriented.

'Do you know what happened, Moira?' Harrison wanted to find the root cause for the fall since it might give them a clue as to what was going on with the woman.

‘I felt a little dizzy.’ She put her hand up to her head and he could see the panic in her eyes as she discovered she was bleeding.

‘I think you banged your head on the way down. When was the last time you had anything to eat or drink, Moira?’ There could be all sorts of reasons behind a person fainting, but the most common cause was low blood sugar. He suspected in a place like this it was easy to lose track of time and forget to eat.

‘I—I can’t remember.’

‘Okay. Could we get the lady some juice, please?’ he asked Gino, hoping to get her something sweet to give her an energy boost.

The floor manager radioed through the request just as another member of staff arrived with the first aid box. Ruby took it from him and set to work cleaning the wound on the side of the woman’s head.

‘This might sting a little but I’ll be as gentle as I can. I just want to clean this up so we can see if you’re going to need stitches.’ Ruby carefully dabbed at the injury, showing the same kindness and understanding she did to everyone. It only made him feel more guilty about leaving her when she’d needed him most. That the one time she’d needed some care and attention she’d been denied it from the one person supposed to love her the most.

She caught him watching her and gave him a little smile. He'd never deserved her, hadn't realized how lucky he was until she was no longer in his life. Now that she was part of it again, he was being made acutely aware of how much she enhanced it simply by being her.

'Unless you have any other health issues we're not aware of, Moira, I think you're suffering from low blood sugar. It's caused you to faint and unfortunately you hit your head. I need you to take a sip of this juice to try and increase your blood sugar levels so you don't pass out again,' he told her. Gino handed him a juice box and Harrison held the straw to the woman's mouth so she could take a sip.

At that moment the paramedics came in and Ruby relayed the relevant information about what had transpired. She seemed to know the older paramedic and introduced him to Harrison as Wyatt Logan. He couldn't help but wonder what their history was, or if they had one.

A surge of irrational jealousy swelled inside him at the easy rapport the two appeared to have. Something she would not be happy about if she was aware. No doubt she would take great pains to point out he had left her, filed for divorce, and disappeared out of her life, so her private affairs were none of his business. It didn't make it any easier for Harrison being reminded of the fact that she would have been with other men in the intervening years, just as he had been with other women. However, he had been the one who'd ended their marriage and he had no right whatsoever to be privy to anything which went on in Ruby's life.

Harrison and Ruby moved back to let the paramedics take over, and in the end they decided to take Moira to the hospital to run some tests and keep her for observation. Leaving Gino thanking them profusely for their help.

'Let me get you some machine credits to thank you,' he said, clearly wanting to show his appreciation in some way.

'That's really not necessary, but thank you. I think we've had enough excitement for one evening.' Harrison shook his hand.

'Well, when you claim your prize we'll make sure to give you the VIP treatment.' With that promise, Gino's radio sparked to life with someone reporting a problem over at the video slots and he rushed off again.

'I think you're right, we should probably call it a night. I'll call a cab,' Ruby said with a yawn.

'I can drive you home. I've only had one beer.' The evening had been full of surprises. Mostly, the feelings towards Ruby which were beginning to re-emerge. It was best that they did call it a night before he got in any deeper.

'Are you sure it's not too much of an inconvenience?'

'Not at all. It will be quicker and safer. I promise. Just give me a minute to leave my details at the reception desk, then we can get out of here.' Harrison led the way back through to the lobby and registered for the prize he'd won. He had no idea if they'd ever claim it, but at least they had a night on the town to look forward to if they should ever want it.

'Well, that was a hell of an evening,' Ruby said on the drive back.

'Not quite what I had planned, but it wasn't dull at least.' The medical drama had provided some distraction from Ruby, even if he'd found himself watching her work and admiring the woman and nurse she'd become. Sad that he'd missed out on being part of her life all this time.

'It definitely wasn't that.' Another yawn and she closed her eyes, settling into the passenger seat, apparently comfortable with him driving.

It felt like the old days. Especially when she fell asleep, her head resting on his shoulder. He didn't even want to disturb her when they pulled up outside her house.

'Ruby? You're home,' he said gently.

'Hmm?' She took her time coming to, blinking awake to stare up at him.

'I said, you're home.' He leaned down closer

and she took the opportunity to snuggle closer into him, shutting her eyes.

Harrison smiled. It was nice having her cuddled up to him again, feeling her warmth against him, her hair tickling his nose. He brushed a strand away from her face. She always looked so peaceful when she slept, and in the mornings he'd wakened her with a kiss. It seemed natural to do it again.

He pressed his lips gently to hers with no intention other than to wake her. Except suddenly Ruby was kissing him back, her hand caressing his cheek and completely undoing him. Since meeting her again it was all he'd wanted to do. To recapture what they'd had before their world had come crashing down around them. However, he knew they were different people and there was a reason he'd done his best to hold back. It hadn't occurred to him that Ruby would have had those same feelings.

Losing loved ones had made him back away from commitment, and getting involved with someone he'd spent the first years of his adult life with was only asking for more heartache. Ruby was absolutely the last person he should be kissing, but it felt so good, so right. Almost as if the last fifteen years hadn't happened. That's why it was so dangerous. He couldn't afford to forget what they'd both been through, or what could happen. Getting close and losing her again in any capacity would be devastating.

So he pulled away, breaking the connection, and ending the moment.

'You're home,' he said, his voice husky with the desire she'd awakened in him by kissing him back so passionately.

Ruby had retreated quickly to her own side of the car, eyes wide open now. 'Sorry. I was half asleep. I forgot where I was for a moment,' she said, the panic evident in her tone.

'Me too,' Harrison said with a half-smile. He should have been full of regret for lapsing, but he couldn't bring himself to be sorry for having one more taste of the woman he'd loved body and soul. At least they both seemed to know it had been a mistake. An accident that they could hopefully put behind them because nothing could come of it. There was too much painful history which had changed his outlook on life forever. During his recovery from that time he'd decided the only way to protect his heart was to keep it closed off. He couldn't afford to let Ruby sneak back in.

'Thanks for the drink. I guess I'll see you around at work.' Ruby was fumbling for the door handle, desperate to escape the close confines of the car. Along with the feelings Harrison had awakened inside her. Want being the one making itself known first and foremost.

Along with embarrassment. She couldn't believe she'd behaved so wantonly where anyone could have seen her. Worse, it had been with Harrison, who'd only come back into her life.

'Goodnight, Ruby,' he said as she slammed the car door shut and hurried towards the apartment. As though putting some distance between them now was going to turn back the clock and somehow prevent that kiss from happening.

She knew he hadn't meant anything by it. It had become a custom of theirs back in the day for him to gently wake her with a kiss. Ruby expected Harrison had been driven by nothing more than a case of nostalgia. She'd been the one to try and turn it into something more.

Muscle memory seemed to have kicked into her entire body, including her libido, when Harrison's lips had met hers, and she'd wanted him. Despite all the pain and heartache he'd put her through, despite the years apart, in that moment they could have been teenagers again. Nothing else mattering except the chemistry between them and the urge to act on it. Thank goodness he'd come to his senses, because she'd seemed to have lost all of hers momentarily.

'Ruby? Is that you?' Her mother appeared and turned the light on, almost blinding her.

'Yes. I'm home.'

Her mother peered closely at her. 'What's wrong? You look upset. Did he do something? I told you to keep your distance from him.'

'What? No. I'm fine. He didn't do anything. We had to deal with a medical emergency, that's all.' It was mostly true. She was the one who'd passionately kissed her ex-husband in the front seat of his car, and currently dealing with a sense of mortification and confusion. Not knowing what had prompted that display, or why she was craving more even when she had come back down to earth.

Her mother narrowed her eyes at her. She had an uncanny knack of being able to see right into Ruby's soul and she didn't want to hang around for her to figure out what had happened. It was going to take a lot for her parents to forgive Harrison, if they ever would, so she definitely wasn't going to understand why Ruby had just been kissing him. Especially when she didn't know herself.

Ruby faked a yawn. 'If Aimee's okay, I think I'll just go on to bed. Thanks for looking after her.'

'Anytime. I'll go and wake your father. He'll be glad you're home safe too.' As Ruby headed towards her bedroom, she could feel her mother's eyes on her back.

She closed the door and collapsed onto the bed, hoping that by tomorrow morning it would all be forgotten. Though she had more than a sneaking suspicion her dreams were going to be dominated by memories of Harrison, old, new and imagined. All fuelled by the fire he'd lit inside her the second he'd touched her lips with his. Prince Charming awakening Sleeping Beauty with one kiss. She'd simply have to try and cling onto the fact that their fairy tale ending had become a living nightmare.

CHAPTER SIX

'HEY, EUGENE. It's Dr Blake. I just thought I'd check in on you.' Harrison had stopped by to visit the boy at the end of his shift. Eugene had already been to theatre and had his burns debrided to remove all of the dead skin and clean out the wounds. Although he was looking better, he still had a long way to go to recovery and remained sedated for now. Eventually he would have to undergo skin grafts to start the healing process, but for now they were simply trying to keep him stable.

Harrison removed some of the dressings to check that there was no infection and, once satisfied, applied some new ones. It wasn't a complete surprise when he saw Ruby coming into the room, and he wondered if part of the reason he'd called here was the hope that their paths might cross. It had been several days since their night out and the kiss in the car and he hadn't seen her since. He wasn't sure if that was by design or accident.

No, he shouldn't have kissed her. That intimate gesture belonged in their past and that had been his mistake. However, he couldn't stop thinking about the way she'd kissed him back. Like no time had passed at all. Like he'd been forgiven for abandoning her and they'd picked up where their relationship had left off before the miscarriage. It was nothing but wishful thinking. They'd both simply been carried away in the moment after a dramatic night. It didn't mean they couldn't be in the same room together. He was sure he could rein his urges in now he'd had some time to think about the complications that getting involved with Ruby again would bring.

They were working together now. With him in a new job, having just moved here. She had Aimee. All things which they couldn't risk, even if she wanted anything more between them than an ill-thought-out kiss. The rate at which she'd fled the car made it pretty obvious she regretted it, so it was doubtful she intended to pursue anything further.

'Hey. How's he doing?' Ruby came straight over to check on Eugene without a hint of awkwardness, so perhaps she'd got over the kiss quicker than he had.

'As well as can be expected. I debrided the wounds, so it's just a matter of how quickly he'll heal. How are you doing? I haven't seen you around for a couple of days.' Without asking her outright if she was avoiding him, Harrison danced around the subject.

'I'm good. Just busy with work and Aimee.' There was no reason he should be a priority in her life, and she obviously had responsibilities, yet Harrison couldn't help but think she could take five minutes to see him if she really wanted to. Perhaps she was regretting having any contact with him at all. The idea that she would rather avoid him now was tough to swallow when he'd got used to having her in his life again already.

'That's good…' They fell into an awkward silence with only the blip of the monitors punctuating it.

'I just thought I'd check in on Eugene before my shift starts, so I suppose I should get moving.'

'Don't let me keep you. I'm on my way home. My clinic's finished for the day.' Harrison clung onto the fact that their shift patterns seemed to be different and that's why he hadn't seen much of her. Obviously she'd been working later.

'Lucky you.'

They both made their way to the door, just as Ruby's cell phone rang. 'Mom? What's wrong?'

It was clear something had happened to warrant a phone call at work, so Harrison hovered nearby in case she needed some help.

'Why didn't you say something before I left? I don't know how I can get away now. No, you need to go to bed. I'll see if I can get someone to cover, though it's late notice.' Ruby hung up with a sigh and a frown.

'Is everything all right?' It was obvious it wasn't but this was the time for her to share if she wanted help.

'Mom and Dad are both sick. They managed to drop Aimee off at school but they can't pick her up. I'm going to have to try and find someone to get her. I can't just leave.' Another heavy sigh as she rubbed her temples.

'I could collect her and take her to your place.' It was out of his mouth before he had time to consider what he was saying. This was the very opposite of keeping his distance from Ruby outside of the hospital, yet it was the obvious solution to her problem.

Ruby looked at him with uncertainty written all over her face. He wasn't sure if he should be offended. 'Are you sure that's not too much of an inconvenience?'

'I have nothing planned. I can swing by and

collect her. As long as you trust me.' He was aware that Ruby wouldn't trust the safety of her daughter to just anyone, and he'd only re-appeared in her life a matter of days ago.

She rolled her eyes. 'Of course I trust you, Harrison. And as you've pointed out, you have a fan in Aimee. However, I don't finish my shift until the early hours of the morning. It's a lot to ask of you to stay with her all night.'

He hadn't realized exactly what he was volunteering for but he wasn't going to let her down now when she was trusting him with the most precious thing in her life. 'It's fine. We'll order a pizza, pop a couple of beers, play a hand or two of poker…'

She slapped him on the arm. 'Seriously, though, I'll be forever indebted to you if you could look after Aimee until I get home. I'll try and get away as early as I can.'

'It's no problem. Just give me the address of the school and a key to your apartment and stop worrying.' Hopefully this would go some way to smoothing over what had happened and put them back on an even keel. They could be friends. Goodness knew when he might need a favour in return.

'Sure. Let me phone the school and make sure they know you're coming. Thanks for this, Harrison.' She flashed him a smile that more than made up for whatever a night babysitting a ten-year-old was going to throw at him.

'Yes, Dr Blake will be picking Aimee up today. Her grandparents are ill and he has my permission to collect my daughter from school. Yes, she knows him. Thank you.' Ruby hung up, glad she'd solved one problem, but hoping she wasn't causing herself more by letting Harrison further into her life. There was no greater responsibility than trusting him enough to look after her daughter and she didn't want to regret it.

She'd purposely tried to keep her distance after that kiss, trying to put it from her mind, expecting that the memory of it would fade away. One glimpse of him and it had all come flooding back. Though he hadn't managed to stay out of her dreams either these past nights. She almost blushed when she'd spotted him because of the X-rated thoughts her subconscious had conjured up during her sleep.

She couldn't be mad at her parents for falling ill, but the timing could have been better. Given her some time to find cover, or someone to babysit who wasn't her ex-husband.

'It's all sorted. The school knows you're coming to pick Aimee up. I can't thank you enough for doing this.' She handed the apartment key over to Harrison, feeling as though she'd just invited him to wreak some more havoc in her life. It was going to be difficult to carry on as normal knowing he'd crossed her threshold, and had become part of the fabric of her home. Where it had only been her and Aimee for as long as she could remember.

'It's no problem. Do I need a list of instructions, or shall I just get her a fake ID and we'll hit the town?' Harrison's insistent teasing wasn't helping calm her nerves.

'Stop! Just make sure she does her homework before dinner, and one hour of TV only. Bed is eight o'clock and don't let her sweet-talk you into anything later or else she'll be grumpy in the morning when I have to wake her for school.' It was likely going to be as odd for Aimee as it was for Ruby to have Harrison in the apartment. She never invited men back to her place, even on the rare occasion she had a date. There was no point disrupting her daughter's life when the relationship would likely never last, and she'd been proved right thus far.

This was different. Aimee had already met Harrison and knew he was Mommy's friend. She had no concept of the complicated dynamic of their past relationship and didn't need to.

Harrison was simply doing them a favour, and there didn't have to be any more to it than that.

'No problem. Hey, stop worrying. It'll be fine.' Harrison did his best to reassure her, likely picking up on her anxiety. Ruby didn't have any qualms about him looking after her daughter, it was simply the implication of letting him cross that line into her personal life again which was causing her concern. Still, she didn't have any choice at present, and she'd be sure to point that out when her mother discovered what was happening.

'Thanks, Harrison. I appreciate this.' She knew he didn't have to do this, he was under no obligation whatsoever, and she was grateful. It was simply perturbing that he'd helped her out so much already within a few days of them getting to know one another again and the last thing she wanted was to come to rely on him. To think of him as part of her and Aimee's life. He'd already proved she couldn't pin her hopes on him because there was always a chance he would disappear again. This time she had Aimee to think of too. It wasn't just her heart on the line.

'Teeth brushed and bed for you, Aimes.' Harrison was looking forward to a rest once his charge was tucked up for the night.

As much as he'd enjoyed her company and been able to help Ruby, he was exhausted. He wasn't used to looking after children all day. Once he'd collected a happy, chatty Aimee from school, they'd been busy all day playing games and working on her art project. Goodness knew how Ruby managed to do this full time on top of her position at the hospital. Of course she had her parents' help, but even so, it was a lot for a person to do on their own.

'Mom always reads me a story.' Aimee emerged from the bathroom in her pyjamas, rubbing her eyes and clearly fighting her tiredness.

'Aren't you a little old for bedtime stories?' He suspected she was just trying to stay up a little later. A ten-year-old's power move that he couldn't deny her.

'It helps me sleep,' she pouted, sealing his fate.

'Okay, then. Into bed.' He stood at the door whilst she chose a book and clambered into bed. Then pulled up the covers around her and perched on the side of the bed.

'I had fun today,' she said, clutching her well-worn teddy bear.

'Me too.' As he said it, Harrison realized as tiring as it had been, he had enjoyed spending time with her. Of course it made him wonder what it would have been like if he had been a father. If he would always have been so patient and fun as he had been with Aimee today. Certainly he'd never intended to be as distant as his own parents had been with him, and from the day Ruby had discovered she was pregnant, he'd sworn to be present and involved with his child. Unfortunately, he'd never had the chance.

'Why do you look so sad?' Aimee was watching him, missing nothing, but it wasn't his place to tell her about his past with her mother.

'I'm just missing my family.' This moment was also bringing back memories of his brother, who'd read to him when he was younger too. Sneaking comics under the covers with a torch and making every bedtime feel like an adventure.

'You can be part of our family,' Aimee said with a smile. 'Then you don't have to be sad anymore.'

He wished it was as simple as that.

'Well, thank you very much. That's made me happier already.' He wasn't sure Ruby would be thrilled with that idea, but it was a nice gesture on Aimee's part to make him feel included. Her kindness and generosity clearly inherited from her mother.

'Will you be coming to get me from school tomorrow?' There was a hope in Aimee's eyes that he hated to extinguish, but he didn't want to promise something and not be able to deliver.

'I don't think so, but I'm sure I will still see you every now and then.' That seemed enough to appease her and she handed over her carefully chosen book before settling down into her bed.

There was a cartoon dog bookmark sticking out of the book and Harrison felt bad for doubting Aimee still had a bedtime story read to her at night. Perhaps it was her way of keeping that bond strong with her daughter when she was working full time. He could just imagine Ruby coming back from a late shift, cuddling up with Aimee on the bed and reading to her until she fell asleep. A heartening scene he almost had a yearning to be part of, because in an alternate reality they both would have been doing that for their own child.

He cleared his throat to try and move the ball of emotion suddenly blocking it. Thoughts of the past, of the future denied him and Ruby, had been uppermost in his mind recently. Likely because of seeing Ruby again and being reminded of it all. It had been easier to try and put those emotions aside when he was simply living the life of a bachelor, not a grieving man who'd lost his baby and left a wife behind.

He'd told himself over the years that he didn't

need a family of his own anymore, that it would cost him his peace of mind worrying that it would all be taken away from him at any point. Being around Aimee and Ruby was showing him what he was missing. Ruby's life was all the richer for having her daughter in it. He couldn't help but think if he'd been stronger, if he'd opened up to his wife sooner, he might have been part of a happy family after all.

Ruby let herself into the apartment and closed the door quietly behind her so as not to disturb Aimee if she was sleeping. She'd half expected to find Harrison on the couch, watching TV, waiting for her to relieve him of his babysitting duties. Apart from the drawings scattered on her coffee table, there was no sign of anyone even being in here.

Then she heard the sound of Harrison's voice drifting from Aimee's room and she smiled, knowing her daughter had conned him into reading to her. She walked towards Aimee's room with every intention of taking over and getting her daughter to go to sleep, but, as she stood in the doorway watching the interaction, she was charmed by the scene.

'Elise took the potion and downed it. It tasted of burnt cabbage and dog food…' Harrison turned up his nose as he read the story.

'Yuck.' Aimee was reading the story over his shoulder but seemed engrossed as much by the reader as the book.

As unnerving as it was to see her ex-husband engaged in a bedtime story with her daughter, it was also quite sweet. Harrison had been robbed of his chance to be a father and she'd always thought it was a role he would have excelled at. Young at heart, patient and kind. All the qualities she'd loved about him were everything needed in a good parent. She should know when she'd been lucky enough to have a mother and father who embodied those very characteristics. It was a shame for her daughter that she hadn't been as fortunate in her own father.

It was little wonder Aimee was making the most of having Harrison around when she'd missed out on that male influence in her life. Ruby's father was always there, of course, when they needed him but it wasn't the same as having someone who'd let her daughter have ice cream for breakfast, or read her bedtime stories.

Afraid that she would get carried away with the sight before her, believing she could still have her happy-ever-after, she turned to leave. However, the movement must have caught Harrison's eye and he glanced up at her.

'Hey.' She walked into the room as though that had been her intention all along.

'Hey, yourself. I wasn't expecting to see you back so soon.' His smile, tired but happy, squeezed her heart like a vise.

'I managed to get some cover.'

'Hi, Mommy.' Aimee stretched out her arms, waiting for the hug she knew was coming.

Harrison got up from the bed and moved aside to give her access to her daughter.

'What are you still doing awake?' Ruby asked, tucking her daughter back under the covers.

'That's my fault, I'm afraid. I got too invested in Elise's adventures.' He waved the book at her, before inserting the bookmark and setting it on the dresser for Ruby to pick up again at another time.

'Easily done.' Ruby grinned back. This was always her favourite part of the day too, spending precious time with her daughter, the outside world locked away until morning.

''Night, Aimee.' Harrison took his leave, letting Ruby say goodnight in private.

'I like Harrison,' Aimee said as Ruby turned off the main light to leave a night light glowing in the corner.

'Me too. Now get some sleep. I'll see you in the morning.' She dropped a kiss on Aimee's forehead, glad she'd been able to get away from work in time to say goodnight.

'Will Harrison be here in the morning?' a little voice asked hopefully in the semidarkness.

'No, sweetheart. He'll be going back to his own house. Now get some sleep.' Ruby blew her another kiss and closed the door.

Aimee's innocent enquiry had taken her by surprise. Not only that she might expect Harrison to spend the night, but also that the thought didn't seem to bother her. It was obvious her daughter was very taken with him and was already seeing Harrison as a friend. The fact brought all manner of questions to mind. Did that mean her daughter was looking for a father figure? That she wouldn't mind if Ruby brought someone home? Or was it just Harrison she was comfortable with being part of their lives?

Up until now Ruby had been very careful about letting men into her daughter's life. Very few had made it, and none recently. She doubted Aimee remembered much of the relationships Ruby had been involved in when she was young, but none had worked out. As a result, Ruby kept that part of her life separate from her daughter. She didn't want to confuse her, or let her get close to people who weren't going to be in her life for very long.

Exactly the reason she should be wary about her getting close to Harrison. Circumstances had already conspired to have him involved in their lives, but theirs was a complicated history she wasn't ready to share with Aimee. If she ever did.

She walked into the living area, her head full of thoughts about Harrison and wondering what harm she could be doing to her family by having him around. Only to find him in the kitchen dishing out a plate of food for her.

'I hope you don't mind. I know you're probably hungry after your shift so I saved you some leftovers. It's just some roast chicken and potatoes.'

'No pizza?' She was stunned that he'd gone to the trouble of actually cooking, never mind saving some for her.

'I'm trying to make a good impression, or at least make up for the whole ice-cream-for-breakfast thing.'

'And Aimee ate this? It's not a judgement on your cooking by the way, but she's a fussy eater. It's difficult to get her to eat anything that isn't shaped like a dinosaur or a smiley face. Please tell me the secret.' Mealtimes had become a battleground, and after a long day at work it was often the last thing she wanted to do, so frequently capitulated to Aimee's requests. It made her feel like a failure as a mother that she couldn't get her daughter to eat healthy, nutritious meals, which as a medical professional, she knew was important for her child's development. Yet, it was processed food which her daughter would eat without a protest. The fact that Harrison, a virtual stranger, had succeeded where Ruby had failed, wasn't helping.

Harrison helped himself to a carrot baton from her plate. 'I don't know what to tell you. We stopped at the store for supplies on the way home. I didn't want to take my eyes off her while I was cooking so I got her to help. She seemed to enjoy preparing a meal. Perhaps you have a budding chef on your hands.'

'Huh.' It gave Ruby some food for thought. She was so focused on sitting down to dinner with her daughter, she never thought about getting her to help cook with her.

'Hey, don't worry about it. I'm just a novelty to her. I'm sure she'd get sick of me and my cooking soon enough given the chance.' He was doing his best to make her feel better about it, yet the image of him here in her house on a regular basis was both exhilarating and terrifying. Ruby was afraid of what she'd already put in motion by letting him help her out to this extent. Showing her daughter that he was someone she could rely on, when Ruby knew from painful experience that wasn't necessarily true.

Yes, she knew now that he'd had his own demons and grief to deal with at the time, but that couldn't take away the pain his actions had caused her. There was nothing to say that in future something in his personal life wouldn't affect her or Aimee. The only way to avoid that was to push him back out of her life. Something which would be easier said than done now.

Especially when it was so nice coming home and having things done for her like this. It was a glimpse at the life they could have had. Were supposed to have had. Managing the childcare between them, having dinner waiting when she came home from work, this was the fairy tale. It was a shame none of it was real. Harrison was simply doing her a favour. Likely trying to make amends for the past, not because this was where he chose to be. He simply hadn't had anything better to do tonight and she'd needed help. There was no point in her reading more into it and hoping something could come of it, because she would only end up disappointed, or worst-case scenario, left heartbroken all over again when he was gone.

'Well, thank you for dinner, Harrison, and everything else.' She didn't know what she would have done without him tonight, and that was the problem.

'You're welcome. Now, if you want to go and have a shower, I can stay on for another half an hour and tidy up the kitchen.' He was already clearing away her plate and wiping down the kitchen surfaces. She wasn't used to anyone but her cleaning, and he hadn't been so domestic when they had lived together. Years of living as a bachelor had clearly had a positive effect on him.

'What are you smiling at?' Harrison caught her moment of reflection.

'I was just thinking about the difference in you since we lived together. It was always you making the mess and me tidying up around you.' The memory that made her smile was now making Harrison wince.

'Sorry about that. I guess I was too immature to be a decent partner to you, Ruby.' He looked genuinely upset and she was sorry she'd even brought up the memory when she knew he'd struggled with his later actions too.

'It's okay, Harrison I've forgiven you for everything. We were both too young to deal with everything that happened. Let's try and put it behind us. Now, if that offer of shower time is still on the table I would really like to take advantage of it. It's not often I get to do that without Aimee knocking on the door.'

She wasn't going to go along with the suggestion, keen to get him out of her apartment before he looked any more at home here, but she hadn't wanted to send him on his way under such a dark cloud. Although it had been difficult, she'd started her life over again after the miscarriage, and he shouldn't feel guilty forever over what had happened. Even if she hadn't realized it at the time, he'd been grieving too. Struggling to cope with the loss as much as she had been, only without the support of family around to get him through.

An extra thirty minutes wasn't going to make much difference to their current situation in the scheme of things.

Ruby took her time showering, enjoying the fact she didn't have to be on alert for Aimee, or have to spend the evening cleaning the kitchen. All she wanted to do after a long shift was veg out on the couch. Thanks to Harrison, it was possible tonight. These past few days he always seemed to be on hand to give her whatever she needed. She knew she couldn't afford to get too used to it. To let her guard down when he might disappear at any given moment, but it was nice to have someone to share the load with for a while at least.

Perhaps she'd be able to return the favour at some point, then she wouldn't feel so indebted to him.

She towel dried and moisturized her body before donning a pair of floral silk pyjamas. With anyone else it might seem a tad awkward, but Harrison had seen her in a lot less and she wanted to be comfortable. Hopefully he would take the hint that she was ready to say goodnight and head home himself.

'Thanks for that, Harrison. It's nice to have a shower without feeling as though I've got a time limit before Aimee gets herself into mischief.' Ruby walked into the living room expecting to see him either cleaning her kitchen or watching TV. He was doing neither.

The sight that greeted her was Harrison fully stretched out on her couch fast asleep. His shirt had ridden up so she could see his flat belly, the beginning of the dark trail of hair she knew intimately. Sudden erotic images of their past flashed behind her eyes. Harrison fully naked. The two of them showering together. Their honeymoon. All passionate encounters she'd tried not to think about these last years because no one and nothing had ever matched up to the times they'd shared.

She was tempted to wake him. To tell him to go home so she didn't have to look at him and be reminded of the good times they'd shared together, but he looked so peaceful she didn't want to disturb him. She reckoned he deserved a rest after a day playing house. As he gave a soft snore, she went and retrieved a blanket from the closet to cover him. Though she hoped he would do the decent thing and leave before Aimee awoke so she didn't get her hopes up that this would become a regular occurrence. The same could be said for Ruby tucking a blanket around him as if she had any right to be this close to him.

She leaned in to kiss his forehead. A simple goodnight kiss he never need know about. Except those full parted lips proved too much temptation. She pressed her lips softly to his for a brief moment, just long enough for her to have sweet dreams thinking about. Before she realized what was happening, Harrison had wrapped an arm around her waist and pulled her down on top of him. She let out a gasp of surprise but it was swallowed by Harrison's mouth on hers. His eyes were closed as he kissed her and she wondered if he was still half asleep. That was, until his hands moved to cup her backside and pull her flush against him, letting her feel every warm, hard inch of him. She sighed into the moment. A long, leisurely kiss that dreams were made of.

It was only when her daughter cried out from her room that Ruby came to her senses.

'Mommy. I don't feel well.'

'I'm coming, honey.' She scrambled off Harrison, embarrassed by her own behaviour, and rushed to take care of her child.

'Please be gone by the time I come back.' Ruby was aware she'd initiated the kiss, that she'd been enjoying it as much as he had, and that was exactly why she had to be so dismissive.

Aimee had to be her number one priority, and there was no way she was going to let her libido, or ancient history, ruin that special relationship.

CHAPTER SEVEN

'TRY AND KEEP the wound dry and covered to minimize the chance of any infection and make an appointment to replace the dressing.' Harrison saw off his last appointment at his day clinic. He was getting ready to finish his shift at the hospital when he got a message for a consultation down in the emergency room about a chemical burn.

He packed up his things and headed down as soon as he could. Time was always a vital factor when it came to treating burns of any description because it could mean the difference not only between full recovery or lifelong scars, but in some cases life or death. Despite the urgency on the patient's behalf hastening his attendance, there was also that possibility of seeing Ruby again which was spurring him on.

There had definitely been a distance between them since that night in her apartment a week ago. She'd made it clear after they'd kissed again that she didn't want things to go any farther. He didn't blame her. Despite all the reasons he knew he shouldn't be with her, every time she touched him he responded solely on a base level. So when she'd kissed him, those urges had flared back to life with a ferocity that had taken them both by surprise.

Neither of them wanted to rekindle the relationship, yet they couldn't seem to avoid the chemistry between them. The night hadn't ended how either of them had imagined and Harrison didn't want her to hate him for their moment of weakness. They still had to work together.

'I got a call about a chemical burn,' he informed the first nurse he encountered in ER.

'Oh, yes, that was Ruby. She thought we should get your opinion. She's through there.' The nurse pointed towards the first cubicle with the curtains pulled around.

At the mere mention of Ruby his stomach did a backflip. He hoped she wouldn't be as cold towards him as she had been when she'd ordered him out of her apartment. Then he realized she was the one who'd called him down here, and he steeled himself to be as professional as possible. Obviously she was willing to put aside personal feelings to consult him and he had to do the same for the sake of the patient.

He whipped the curtain back with the confidence of the expert he was in his field. However, his bravado faltered when he saw her standing next to the patient's bedside. She looked so pale, so thin, he was automatically concerned for her. Had he caused this by coming back into her life? Upsetting her to the point that she looked ill? The thought didn't sit well with him and it was clear he needed to talk to her to find out what had happened and what she wanted him to do. He might have to reconsider his position here if this was the effect his presence was having on her physically.

'This is Dr Blake. He's a burns specialist. I wanted him to consult on your treatment, Mr McQueen, to make sure you have the best possible outcome.' She gave Harrison a half-smile, which went some way to reassuring him that she didn't despise the very sight of him at least.

'Hello, Mr McQueen. Can you tell me what happened?' It was an opportunity for the patient to bring the doctor up to speed on the events leading up to his admittance into the emergency room.

'I splashed some potassium hydroxide into my eyes at work. I tried to wash it out, but my vision is limited.' The fear in the young man's voice was evident and rightly so. Losing his sight permanently was a very real possibility.

'We've irrigated the eyes and applied antibiotic eye drops. I just wanted you to take a look at his eyelids as he's having trouble closing them,' Ruby added, clearly wanting the best outcome possible for her patient.

'May I take a look for myself?'

Ruby stepped aside to give him access to the patient's bedside and he carefully examined the affected eye and surrounding area. Turning the eyelid inside out to make sure there was no foreign object causing further irritation.

'Although the eyelid is swollen at present, I don't think it needs surgery. It should subside. However, I'd like to send him to ophthalmology for a thorough examination, Nurse Jones. Then I think if we can find him a private room somewhere we can keep the lights dimmed, it would help.' The bright fluorescent lights of ER were a help to the medical staff, but in this case it could exacerbate the patient's problem.

'I'll set that up now.' Ruby walked away to make the necessary phone calls but he didn't want to leave without checking on her welfare too. She did not look well.

'Am I going to lose my sight, Doc?' the patient asked, not knowing which way to direct his question.

'We will do everything in our power to try and prevent that. For now, just rest, and we'll get you some pain relief and dilating eye drops to help with your discomfort, Mr McQueen.'

'Thanks, Doctor.' The man settled back into the bed, though Harrison knew it would be hard for him to relax until he was able to see anything other than darkness.

Harrison caught up with Ruby at the nurses' station.

'Thanks for that. I just wanted to make sure we're giving him the best opportunity of recovery,' she said, leaning against the desk.

'Of course. That's what I'm here for. Are you okay, Ruby? You don't look so well yourself.' Up close he could see beads of sweat forming on her forehead.

'I feel a little hot.' She was swaying so much now he was forced to reach out and steady her.

'Can someone get me a chair for Nurse Jones, please?' A porter passing through immediately pushed a chair beneath her just as she collapsed into it.

'I got you some water, Ruby. You don't look so good. You should go home.' One of the nurses handed her a paper cup as it soon became apparent to everyone that she wasn't well.

'I can't. I'm on the late shift,' she protested.

'Ruby, if you've got any sort of stomach flu you can't be around the patients. You know that. Let me take you home. I'm finished for the day.'

Harrison knew that she wouldn't go home for her own sake but there was no way she would put her patients at risk.

'Okay.' Her soft acceptance told him everything he needed to know about how ill she was, not fighting him over his offer.

It wasn't long before they managed to gather her things and make sure cover was in place before he helped her out to the car.

'I just feel so weak. It's probably the same virus my parents and Aimee had. I thought I would escape.' She gave him a weak smile as he pulled the seat belt around her before he got into the driver's seat beside her.

'No such luck. You need to rest up.'

They were only five minutes away from the hospital when Ruby grabbed his arm. 'You need to pull over, Harrison.'

'What's wrong?'

'I think I'm going to be sick.'

Ruby opened the car door the minute he pulled over to the side of the road, and retched. His heart went out to her, knowing this was the last thing she wanted. Never mind being sick, but being with him at her most vulnerable, fragile state would not have been her choice.

All he could do was rub her back and offer words of comfort as her shoulders heaved. When it subsided and she sank back into her seat he handed her a bottle of water to rinse her mouth out.

'Better?' he asked, his forehead knitted in concern.

She shook her head, her eyes watering. 'Not really.'

'We're not far from my house. Why don't we take you back there until you're feeling better?'

She nodded.

'What about Aimee? Is she being taken care of tonight?'

'Mom has her.'

'Okay, then, that's settled.' Harrison got the car moving again, his mind already made up that he was going to take care of her. There was no way he was going to let her go home on her own when she was so ill. He'd let her down before when she needed him and he wasn't going to do it a second time. He was going to be there for her.

Ruby was too ill, too weak, to argue with Harrison. He was her white knight, once again riding in with a lift home and an offer to help that she couldn't refuse. She hadn't felt one hundred percent when she'd started her shift but thought she was simply tired after running around after her parents and Aimee during their bout of sickness. It was only when she'd seen Harrison's look of concern in that cubicle that she realized she was in real trouble. Now there was absolutely no denying she was ill. All she wanted to do was collapse into bed. Right now, she didn't care whose.

That last night in her apartment when she'd kissed Harrison had been reason enough to stay away from him. Every time they were alone things got dangerously out of control where their libidos were concerned.

It was ridiculous she should have missed him these past days when he'd only been back in her life for such a short time, but he'd made his mark on her again. Aimee too, who hadn't stopped asking about him since. Ruby had almost been disappointed when she'd wakened the next morning to find the blanket neatly folded on the Harrison-free couch, regardless that she'd told him to leave.

Now that she was sick she was glad she had someone to lean on for the time being. There was no one at home and she wasn't sure how she would manage on her own when she was as weak as a kitten. As soon as she was feeling better she'd be out of here.

They pulled up outside Harrison's house, and though her head felt too heavy to lift she did take the time to view the surroundings. For all intents and purposes, it looked like a family home, not a bachelor pad. A charming two-story property with a garage and a garden in a family neighbourhood. Far too big for one man on his own. She couldn't help but wonder if he had aspirations of a family at some point in his life. Although she would be happy for him to move on from their painful past, the thought of him having that happy family they were denied caused a sharp stabbing pain in her heart.

'Let me get that for you.' Mistaking her hesitation as something to do with her illness perhaps, he reached across and undid her seat belt, before stretching farther across her to open the door.

That close personal contact still able to thrill her even when she felt at her worst.

'Thanks.' She followed him up onto the porch of the house and, while she waited for him to open the door, she looked down and saw the evidence of her spectacular display on the roadside down the front of her shirt.

'Oh, no. It's in my hair too,' she cried, horrified.

'Don't worry, we can get your clothes in the wash and I'll run you a bath.' Harrison's bright smile was in stark contrast to how dreadful she felt, and probably looked. As well as the nausea and the hot and cold sweats, she just felt dirty.

'Thanks, Harrison. I'm so sorry I'm imposing on you again.' If she had any girlfriends she would have called on them for help, but motherhood and a demanding job meant her social life suffered. She didn't see many colleagues outside of work except for the odd birthday meal or drink. There was no one close enough for her to lean on at times like this other than her parents and they were already babysitting across town for her.

If Harrison was someone she'd just met at work, she would never have dreamed of coming back to his place, much less strip out of her dirty clothes. It was that past relationship she kept trying to distance herself from that made her trust him. He'd always been good at taking care of her, even when she was sick, and that made her lean in to his offer.

During those early stages of her pregnancy when morning sickness and heartburn had been the bane of her life, Harrison had been there making her dry toast for breakfast. Making sure she had whatever pregnancy-safe remedies he could find to help ease her symptoms. He'd got her through the worst days when it all seemed too much and she was tired of feeling so sick all the time.

That was why his sudden disappearance after the miscarriage had hurt all the more. He was the one person she thought would be there to make her feel better, to tell her everything was going to be okay. But he wasn't.

'If you want to take off those dirty clothes, there's a robe in my bedroom you can use. I'll run you a bath, then we'll see if we can find you something to wear until your things are washed and dried.' He led her through the house where the white walls and tiled floor made it seem so modern and new compared to the homely exterior.

The white theme continued into his bedroom. 'I think I'm going to end up with snow-blindness,' she joked feebly.

'I know. I haven't had the chance to put my own stamp on things yet, or unpacked everything.' He moved a few boxes on the floor so she had a clear way through.

It was unsettling seeing a huge bed and nothing else except the two of them in the room.

'I'm sure you'll get things the way you want eventually. It's a nice place you've got.'

'Thanks.' He opened the closet where his shirts and pants were hanging, retrieved his robe and handed it to her. 'The bathroom's just across the hall. I'll run you a bath and leave you to it. If you need anything, just shout.'

With that, he made a hasty exit, closing the door behind him. Legs weak, she perched on the end of his bed to undress, noting the few personal items on his bedside dresser.

Some loose change, his watch, the same aftershave he'd worn when they were teenagers and, most notably, a ceramic cactus she'd painted for him on a craft evening they'd gone to on a date once. The sort of place that provided ready-made dishes and ornaments for you to decorate before glazing them for you. He'd painted a ceramic unicorn for her, which, at the height of her anger after he'd left, she'd thrown at the wall and watched shatter into smithereens.

Once she'd stripped and folded her clothes into a pile, she donned his robe and shifted her position on the bed so she could take a better look at the battle-weary cactus. The paint was chipped and it was missing a few spikes, but the fact that he'd kept it was touching. It wasn't a practical item, so he hadn't kept it for any other reason than nostalgia. Just as she couldn't resist spraying a little of his aftershave on the robe. The smell transported her back to their early dates, and the nerves she'd felt waiting for him after school. Even now the scent did something to her.

There was a knock on the bedroom door. 'The bath's ready when you are.'

'Thanks.' Ruby sprang to her feet, as though

she'd been caught doing something she shouldn't. Like going through his personal belongings.

Before she was tempted to rummage through any more of his things, she crossed the hall to the bathroom and left her pile of clothes outside the door.

The steamy bathroom was filled with the scent of lavender. The tub full of bubbles. Just how she liked it. He knew everything she liked, and she'd forgotten how nice it was to have someone who anticipated what she needed. That was the good part of a relationship. She'd been so focused on the reasons she should avoid getting close to anyone, the pros of having a partner had been resigned to history. A small gesture like this had a way of transforming a bad day into a nice time.

As she stripped off and sank into the suds, she wondered if it was time to open her life back up to someone again. She closed her eyes and relaxed into the hot, soapy water. Despite the nausea, and that awful anticipation of when it might strike again, this was the most relaxed, most pampered she'd felt in a long time. It was all thanks to Harrison.

He used to do this for her in the old days when it was her time of the month, or if she'd had a particularly rotten day. A warm bath, some soothing music, and he'd wash her hair for her. Making her feel loved. The only person other than her parents or her daughter who'd managed that.

'Ruby? Are you okay in there?' Harrison called through the door, probably to make sure she hadn't passed out and drowned.

'I'm fine.'

'Do you need anything?'

'Could you…could you wash my hair?' She knew it was asking a lot, of both of them. Taking them somewhere they weren't supposed to go. An intimate act she would never ask of a stranger, but Harrison was much more than that no matter how hard they tried to fight it. Right now she was feeling sorry for herself and simply needed a little tender loving care.

It was a hot minute before he responded. 'Are you sure?'

'Please, Harrison.' She was tired, sick and emotional, and just wanted a little comfort.

As the handle on the door moved, she grabbed a hand towel and covered her chest, then scooped the bubbles around her to preserve her modesty. Regardless that Harrison was familiar with her naked body.

'Are you feeling any better?' he asked, seeming a little perturbed by her request. Ruby realised then what she was asking of him. She had no right to expect him to perform such an intimate act when they were no longer married, simply because she was feeling lonely and vulnerable.

'Just feeling sorry for myself. You don't have to do this. I shouldn't have asked.'

'No, it's okay. I know this used to make you feel better, I just want to make sure you're all right with me coming in here like this.'

'I asked you to, didn't I?' It was sweet of him to make sure she was in her right mind, that she wouldn't regret asking him to do this, but it was all she wanted at this moment.

'It's been a long time since I did this.' He rolled up his sleeves and kneeled at the side of the bath.

The admission warmed Ruby, knowing that this was something just between them. It wasn't part of any seduction routine he used with other women. Their secret love language that even now showed how much he still cared for her.

He scooped the water over her hair, slicking it back with his hands. That gentle touch soothing her to the point of near sleep. Eyes closed, she listened to the sound of a bottle opening, then the scent of raspberries filling the air before Harrison's hands were in her hair lathering the shampoo. He took his time massaging her scalp, his fingers firm but tender. Unknotting all the tension in her body with his touch. All too soon it seemed, it was over. He was rinsing out the suds with the same care, making sure none of the water splashed over her face.

'I've left some towels, and a T-shirt and some sweatpants for you. I'll go and make us something to eat and let you get dressed.' Harrison let her know her private head massage was over and left the bathroom.

Ruby sighed, so relaxed she could have melted into the bubbles. She hadn't realised how much she missed the touch of another person. Or was it Harrison's in particular that she missed? He'd been her safe place, her sanctuary for such a long time, it was easy to get comfortable with him again. Deep down she knew that was asking for trouble, but for tonight at least, she simply needed a little comfort.

She was almost asleep, the bath water cooled now, when Harrison called through to let her know dinner was ready. Although she was feeling better, she didn't have much of an appetite. Since he'd gone out of his way to take care of her tonight the least she could do was keep him company as he ate.

She dried off and slipped into the clothes he'd left her. The oversize casual wear was so comfortable it felt like slipping into a Harrison hug. As close as she was likely to get these days.

'I just made us some chicken soup. I thought

that might help settle your stomach a little. Sit down and I'll bring it over to you.' Harrison in the kitchen was becoming a common sight for her, along with having him looking after her. She knew she should fight against it before she got too used to it, but it was so nice she couldn't find the strength to protest.

'You're really spoiling me tonight.' Ruby took a seat at the dining table and waited for Harrison to join her.

'You deserve it. Plus, I don't really get a chance to have company for dinner. You're the first person I've had over.' He set down a bowl of delicious-smelling homemade soup and a plate of bread. She'd half expected him just to open a tin and heat it on the stove but he'd gone that extra mile. If he was trying to impress her, it was working.

'Surely you cook for other women.' Okay, it was a fishing exercise. She was curious about his personal life and his past relationships since her. It was only natural to wonder who else he'd done this for.

He screwed up his face. 'Not really. I tend to eat out if I have a dinner date. I like to keep things casual.'

'Oh. Okay.' Ruby contemplated that information as she ate her soup. A couple of things struck her. Firstly, that she was receiving special treatment, but also that he wasn't a fan of serious relationships. It hadn't seemed that way when they'd been together, when they'd been making plans for the future. The idea that he didn't want to be tied to anyone made her question if he'd decided that during their marriage or after it. Did it partially explain why he'd left, or, like her, had he been too burned to fully invest in another partner?

'What about you? Did you ever come close to marrying again?' The whole scene should have seemed absurd for her ex-husband to be asking about her love life while she was sitting having dinner with him wearing his clothes. Then again, she'd just had a bath in his house, with him washing her hair for her. The truth was, they'd always had such an easy relationship that even after their years apart they'd fallen into that same groove. Where everything felt natural.

Ruby shook her head. 'I was with Aimee's father for a while obviously, but he didn't stick around once I found out I was pregnant.'

'I'm sorry.'

She shrugged. 'There was no question of me keeping the baby. I wasn't going to lose another child, and he showed his true colours. It's just been me and Aimee since. I've dated on and off but I don't want to confuse her by bringing men home. Besides, I'm too busy with work to have room for a social life.'

'We're a sad pair, aren't we?' he said with a laugh.

'Speak for yourself. I'm very happy with my life.' Ruby bristled. Then she remembered how much advantage she was taking by being here. 'In saying that, it is nice to have someone run me a bath and cook me dinner.'

Tonight had opened her eyes to so many possibilities. Like perhaps dating again so she could have someone look out for her for a change. There was also the fact that she could still have Harrison in her life without the world falling apart. It was clear they had a bond which would take years to form with someone else. As long as they kept things platonic, perhaps she wouldn't have to distance herself from him completely.

Yes, she'd given in to temptation and kissed him, but she was hoping that was simply a hang-over from their past. It was so easy being with him that sometimes she forgot they weren't still together. If she opened herself up to the possibility of being with someone else, perhaps Harrison would no longer have such a hold on her.

'My turn next,' he said with a grin.

Though he was only joking, the thought of him in her bath at home, with her washing his hair, was beginning to raise her temperature again. She moved her focus to her soup, doing her best to stop thinking of him in that way before she had to place a total ban on him being in her life. Tonight was proving how much she liked having him back in it. She would simply have to keep her pervy thoughts to a minimum.

'Thank you so much for that,' she said, pushing her empty bowl aside, feeling like a fraud now that her sickness seemed to have passed.

'You're very welcome. Now, your favourite film is on tonight if you want to watch it?' If Harrison had been planning a seduction, he couldn't have done it better, but Ruby knew he was just being kind. It was his way of trying to make it up to her over the past and she had to say, it was working. With every kind gesture, he was reminding her of the man she'd loved, who'd taken such good care of her. Not the one who'd left her heartbroken and grieving on her own.

Harrison didn't want to move. Ruby was asleep on his shoulder, curled up on the couch beside him. He'd never expected her to go along with any of this tonight, but it had proved how out of sorts she was to agree, and how much she'd needed some TLC.

It had felt good to do something nice for her,

but he'd be lying if he said it wasn't a struggle for him to keep his feelings at bay. He was doing his best to be there as support, but with every minute they spent together, he was reminded of how it used to be between them. How he felt about her. And that wasn't what either of them needed right now. The bath, dinner and watching her favourite romcom were moments from the past, and as nostalgic as it was, there was no going back.

Here and now, Ruby was simply a sick friend and colleague who needed a good night's sleep. Preferably without him thinking about what the next step used to be after a bath and a cuddle on the couch.

'Ruby?' He gently tried to wake her.

'Hmm?' She began to stir.

'I think you'd be more comfortable in bed. Come on.' He scooped her up into his arms, feeling her slender frame through the baggy clothes she'd been forced to wear.

Strong, capable, confident Ruby wrapped her arms around his neck and nuzzled into him. The fragile woman he knew she could be sometimes beneath the surface. He wondered about the last time she'd been so vulnerable with anyone else, and silently thanked her for letting him offer her comfort this time. Knowing he'd let her down in the past. It took a great deal of trust for her to let her guard down like this and he was honoured. He just hope he deserved it.

Harrison carried her through to his bedroom and set her down on the mattress. He pulled the covers over her and turned to leave.

'Where are you going?' Ruby mumbled sleepily.

'I'll make up a bed on the couch. You get some sleep and I'll see you in the morning.' With Aimee staying at her grandparents' place for the night anyway it made sense for Ruby to stay here in case she needed help.

'Stay.' She patted the bed.

'I don't think that's a good idea, Ruby…'

'Look, we've already proved we can be around one another without doing too much damage. You washed my hair for goodness' sake. For one night I just want to sleep with someone next to me.'

'You just want some company?' It was going to be a serious test of his restraint to sleep in the bed next to her without reaching for her, but all she was asking was a favour. The least he owed her.

'Be my big spoon,' she said with a pleading smile that made it hard for him to say no to.

It would have been odd for him to get into bed fully clothed, so Harrison did what he usually did going to bed, and stripped down to his boxers. Ruby turned away so he could cuddle up behind her. He slung an arm around her waist and she wriggled back against him so her curvy behind was pressed perilously close against him. Sleep was not going to come easy.

CHAPTER EIGHT

For a split second upon waking up, Ruby thought she'd been caught in a time-slip. She was in bed with her husband and living her happy-ever-after. It was crushing when reality came rushing back to remind her that they were divorced and he was only in bed because she'd begged him to get in beside her.

She cringed at the memory, blaming it on feeling so sick and vulnerable at the time. Simply wanting more of that familiar comfort he'd been providing for her all night. It had been nice falling asleep in his arms, even nicer opening her eyes to see him next to her. She missed this. Being part of a couple, having someone there for her, instead of being on her own. More than that, she missed having all of that with Harrison.

She watched him sleep. So peaceful. So handsome. He was bare-chested, displaying a more mature, muscular physique than the teen

Harrison she'd married. It took everything in her not to reach out and touch him, yearning for the sort of closeness and intimacy they'd once had.

His eyes fluttered open and when he saw her watching him, a lazy grin spread across his face, making her pulse flutter.

'Morning,' she said, trying to control her impulse to kiss him.

'How are you feeling?' The fact that it was his first question, his concern for her uppermost in his thoughts, said a lot about him.

'Good. Thank you. I'm sorry if I put you in a difficult situation. I guess I was just feeling sorry for myself.' Although Harrison looked comfortable being in bed with her, she could see now it had been a big ask from his ex-wife. She hadn't really given him a chance to say no regardless of how uncomfortable he might have felt about it.

'It's fine. Best sleep I've had in ages.'

They were so relaxed together in that moment that Ruby voiced what was on her mind. 'Why couldn't we have saved us, Harrison?'

She saw the pain flicker across his face. The same thing she felt every time she thought about what they'd lost. Last night had helped her remember all the good times they'd had together. How great they'd been as a partnership, and how safe he'd made her feel. He still had that same ability, and it was becoming clear that now her anger towards him was dissipating, she still cared for him as much as she ever had.

He let out a heavy sigh before shifting his position so he was sitting upright, the covers falling down to his lap to give her a front-row view of his muscular torso. But now wasn't the time to be ogling her ex-husband, who appeared to be gearing up for a serious conversation. Ruby sat up beside him, their easy, lazy morning apparently over.

Harrison couldn't seem to block out the inner voice shouting, *Tell her*, in his ear. She'd put so much trust in him last night by letting him take care of her, he wanted to do the same in return. To open up and finally tell her about his brother, and why the miscarriage had devastated him to such an extent that he'd ended their marriage. She deserved a full explanation and he felt close enough to her right now for her to be the one person he felt comfortable confiding in.

'I wasn't completely honest with you about the reason I left, Ruby.'

He felt her bristle beside him and knew he had to expand before she got the wrong idea. 'I was crushed by losing the baby, and I did fall into a deep depression, that's all true. But I never told you the whole story.'

'I'm listening,' she said softly, her big blue eyes watching him, waiting for the truth.

It would be so much easier simply to kiss her again, because they had a habit of forgetting everything else when they were lost to the passion between them, but this felt like the right time to have that conversation he'd been avoiding for too long.

Last night, cuddled up next to her, feeling the soft curve of her behind pressed against him had been torturous, but also comforting. He'd forgotten what it was like to be so close to someone, physically…and emotionally. These past years he'd been so determined to protect himself, relationships had been casual, so when they ended it didn't hurt so much. That meant sleepovers were kept to a minimum, and he certainly didn't run baths, cook dinner and just cuddle with anyone else in his life. Ruby did, and probably always would, hold a special piece of his heart.

He wished he'd been able to share everything about the loss of his brother with her, but it had been too painful and he hadn't wanted to seem weak. Then, when everything had come crashing down, he hadn't wanted to burden her with that extra layer of grief he'd been struggling with. Now, however, he could see how much that had contributed to the breakdown of their marriage. That lack of communication, that inability to admit he needed help, let her think the worst of him. He didn't know what the future held for them but it was time to open up about the part of his life he'd kept to himself for too long.

'When we lost the baby it brought back a lot of unhappy memories for me. Something I never told you, never told anyone, was that I lost my big brother, Joey, when I was eleven years old.' Saying the words alone felt like a weight lifted from his shoulders, even if his voice still wobbled when he spoke about it.

'You had a brother? We've known each other for years. Been married for goodness' sake. Why couldn't you tell me?' The disbelief in Ruby's voice was to be expected. They'd shared so much with each other and been such a big part of one another's lives. It must feel like a betrayal of sorts that he'd kept that information from her.

His parents, divorced by then, hadn't really been an active part of his life. Harrison had spent most of his time at Ruby's family home when they were younger, so it had been easy to avoid the subject. He'd never outright lied, and like Ruby, most people assumed he was an only child. Something he'd never corrected when it would have meant pouring out the whole tragic story, which was too hard for him to do. It was easier for him to try and set aside that dark time of his life rather than talk about it. At least, until they lost the baby, then everything seemed to have hit him at once.

'I'm sorry. It was just too difficult for me to talk about him. I idolised Joey. He was more of a parent to me than Mom and Dad ever were. Always looking out for me.' Harrison couldn't help but smile. Telling her that brought back some of the happier memories he often forgot when all he could remember was how bereft he'd been left after his brother's death.

After a minute of silence, Ruby finally asked, 'What happened?'

That meant Harrison having to face the bad memories again. He closed his eyes, picturing that night. Sitting at the top of the stairs, seeing the coloured lights from the police car shining through the front door, listening to his parents' wails of anguish, and knowing life would never be the same.

'It was a hit and run driver. He was walking home from a party and killed instantly.'

'I'm so sorry, Harrison.' Ruby was such an empathetic person he could see his own pain reflected in her teary eyes. It gave him some comfort that she understood how hard it had been for him then, and now.

'Did they ever get who did it?'

He shook his head. That had been as difficult to accept as losing his brother. That someone had robbed him of his best friend and got away with it, never brought to justice and able to get on with the life Joey had been denied.

'Unfortunately not. It was likely another partygoer who'd been drinking. There were no witnesses, no evidence. Just my brother lying at the side of the road in the rain.' His voice broke as he was forced to imagine that scene again. His big brother cold and alone, not knowing how much his little brother wished he'd been there with him to hold his hand and tell him how loved he'd been.

'Then you never got closure.'

'I guess not. It destroyed my parents. They split up and I moved away with my mom. You know the rest.' He gave her as much of a smile as he could muster. Meeting Ruby had been his redemption. Given him something to live for again. Made him feel loved again.

'Why didn't you tell me?' she asked softly.

'I just couldn't. It was too painful. We didn't talk about him at home anymore and I just didn't know how to handle that overwhelming grief and sense of loss. It was easier to pretend that part of my life had never happened.' It almost felt like a betrayal to have wiped those early years hanging out with Joey and simply being a kid. After his death, Harrison was forced to grow up, the innocence of his childhood over.

'We were married, Harrison. Supposed to be a family. How could you keep that part of you closed off from me?'

He was ashamed of himself for being so weak that he felt he couldn't share that part of him. The sadness, the hole in his heart he didn't imagine that even Ruby could fix, so he didn't want to burden her with it.

'I—I thought I had to be the strong one in the relationship. I didn't want you to see that side of me. To think less of me. Then it went on for so long it never seemed right to tell you. I knew you'd be upset and it was easier just to keep that part of my life to myself. I'm sorry.' In hindsight, that was probably what had ultimately destroyed their relationship. His inability to open his heart fully to Ruby because it hurt too much to confront that part of his life. Something he'd only dealt with when it had been too late to save their marriage.

'I'm sorry you felt you couldn't share that with me.'

'I suppose I was acting the way my parents

had by trying to just shut it out. Then when the miscarriage happened—'

'It all came flooding back.' Ruby understood. As she always would have if he'd been brave enough back then to let her in.

'I'm sorry I wasn't there for you. I know I've said it before, but I hope you understand why. I can't change what happened, or how I acted—'

'Ssh.' Ruby put her finger on his lips. 'I understand. I do. That grief of losing the baby was double for you because you hadn't fully dealt with losing your brother.'

'I just…yeah, I'm sorry.'

'I guess it helps knowing that. Not that you were suffering so much, but that it wasn't because you just wanted out of the relationship.'

'Definitely not. It killed me staying away, but in the end, I thought you'd be better off without me. I'd left it too long to go back, and just couldn't find the words to express what I was going through. It was never you. You were the only good thing in my life.' Losing Ruby too, on top of everything else, had been what had tipped him over the edge, regardless that it had been his own doing. And now she was back in his life, in his bed, he knew he was treading a dangerous path.

Ruby leaned her head against his shoulder and took his hand in hers. 'I wish we'd been able to talk about this before now. I spent years being angry at you, and blaming myself that I hadn't been enough for you to stay.'

'That was never the case.'

Her sad smile up at him was heartbreaking. 'But I didn't know that, did I? I didn't know that neither of us were to blame, or that you were working through such difficult personal issues aside from our own loss.'

'Because I didn't tell you.' He nodded.

'Right, and we've wasted all this time bogged down in the past when all we needed was to talk.' The pain in her eyes was difficult to see when he knew he was responsible for putting it there. It was Harrison's fault he hadn't told her about Joey and how much his death had affected him. He didn't know what he hoped to gain from telling her now other than closure when it was too late for their relationship.

'I guess then you wouldn't have Aimee.' He could never have denied her the chance to be a mother, even if it meant that he wasn't part of that family. There was no way of telling how things would have panned out if they'd managed to save their relationship, and he couldn't punish himself forever over what had happened. He simply had to accept it.

'True. I just… I loved you, you know.' Ruby

didn't have to tell him, he did know. That's what had broken his heart.

'I loved you too.' He didn't think he'd ever stopped.

Ruby looked up at him, her gaze full of regret, and what he thought was a longing to relive the good times they'd shared. It seemed right to bend down and kiss her. To lean into that bond they'd created all those years ago, but which hadn't seemed to dissipate. The soft touch of her lips felt like home. A time when everything had been good. When he was happy. Something he thought he'd never be again after Joey died. It was easy to imagine they were back there, carefree in their love nest. Especially when she was wrapping her arms around his neck, deepening the fantasy with him.

Before he knew it she was straddling his waist, making sure his whole body was wide awake.

'Are we really going to do this?' he mumbled against her lips, aware there would be consequences later of giving in to temptation now.

She put her finger on his lips again. 'Shh.'

An indication that she didn't want to think beyond this moment, and if Harrison was honest, neither did he. Because then he'd have to stop Ruby from kissing him the way she was right now. His face cupped in her hands, and her mouth latched onto his. Every flick of her tongue against his fuelling his desire and eroding any reason for putting a stop to this.

Ruby stripped off his sweatshirt, revealing her body to his lusting gaze. Motherhood had given her a fuller, womanly figure and he was here for it. Her full breasts pressed close to his chest as she continued to kiss him, desire overtaking every thought except the need for one another.

Harrison took possession of her breasts in the palms of his hands, kneading, massaging, hearing her gasp, seeing her close her eyes and give in to the sensation. He flicked his tongue over her nipple, teasing until it was puckered and standing to attention. Ready for him to take fully in his mouth, sucking, grazing to tip with his teeth, until she was bucking against him with want.

Harrison wasn't sure if this moment was something borne of nostalgia, or an exploration of potentially something new. What he did know was that he didn't want it to end. He'd never had a physical relationship with anyone like the one he'd had with Ruby. Likely because they had that emotional connection he did his best to avoid making these days. They'd loved one another. Deep down, he knew that love was still there. Mixed in with that passion which had been reawakened with their first touch, it made for an explosive time in the bedroom. Something it seemed they were both keen to revisit.

Harrison grabbed her by the hips and rolled her over so he was on top. Their bodies entwined, but that frustrating barrier of fabric prevented them from being completely as one.

He whipped down the loose sweatpants in one smooth action, with Ruby helping to kick them away. Her hands were on the waistband of his boxers pushing them out of the way, and releasing him fully to her exploration. That feeling of her first touch felt like letting out a too-long-held breath. As though he'd been waiting for it, needing it to survive.

Ruby took hold of his erection, claiming it with a possessive hand that made him gasp. And when she moved it up and down his shaft he thought he might explode. If this was the only time he got to be with her, he was going to make sure it would be one to remember for both of them. For all the right reasons.

He grabbed hold of her hand, then the other, before pinning them to the bed above her head. Ruby's eyes glittered as she watched him move his way down her body, pressing feather-light kisses across her skin. Teasing them both.

He felt her tense when he reached her belly,

squirming as he released her hands from his grasp and dipped lower.

'Harrison…' It was a plea for him to relieve her frustration and he was only too willing to oblige.

Moving farther down the bed, positioned between her legs, he licked a path along her inner thigh. Her little groan of pleasure helping to steel his own arousal.

And when he lapped her core with the flat of his tongue, and dipped inside her, he was nearly undone himself. Her arousal was instant, as though she too had been waiting for this moment for too long.

In no time at all she was quivering beneath him, crying out as her climax came at his behest. Harrison couldn't wait any longer for his own satisfaction and once he'd donned a condom, he slid easily inside her with one thrust. Her tight heat encompassed him as he joined their bodies together. He felt uncharacteristically emotional about reconnecting this way with Ruby, but channelled that swell of emotion into a physical display to show her how much he still cared for her. Taking his time to make her feel as good as he did. Doing his best to erase those difficult memories and replace them with all new erotically charged ones.

With her limbs wrapped around him, clinging to him as though her life depended on it, Ruby climbed that peak of ecstasy with Harrison. And when he finally surrendered to that ultimate satisfaction, she came with him for a second time. Her body quivering and tensing, before finally turning liquid around him.

He wanted to stay here forever, pretending that they'd never parted. That they hadn't gone their separate ways, or led completely different lives. He'd never regretted what had happened more between them in the past than he did right now. Knowing he could have had this forever, sharing more than his bed and his body with someone. Being part of someone else's life, and having Ruby be part of his on a permanent basis. The reminder of what he'd been missing out on with her for all of these years cut deep.

Harrison lay down beside Ruby on the bed with a sigh.

'What's wrong?' she asked, pulling the bedsheet up to cover her nakedness, her brow knitted into a worried frown.

He was tempted to pretend he was fine, that he was the carefree happy bachelor he portrayed to everyone else, but he didn't want to lie to Ruby. Keeping his feelings from her had been what had caused their split in the first place. If he wanted her to be in his life again in any capacity, this time around he had to be open with her.

'I just… I don't know. Tonight's made me nostalgic I suppose for the life we used to have together.' He knew there was no point in looking back when they couldn't change the past, and he'd already told her that he didn't begrudge her going on to have her own family. It didn't mean he wasn't pining for that lost time.

Ruby shifted over and laid her head on his chest, her body pressed against his side. 'We can't live life with regret, Harrison. It's difficult enough.'

'I guess I'm just wondering what happens next. If this is it.' Now they'd rekindled that passionate fire, it would be hard to put it out and forget it had ever sparked to life. It would be impossible to see her at work and pretend this had never happened. That he didn't want her with every fibre of his being.

Harrison didn't want to sound needy, but this was a big deal to him. Being with Ruby was completely different to spending the night with anyone else. There was a lot more at stake, and he needed to know for his own peace of mind what he might be getting himself into. Either to prepare himself for disappointment if this thing between them didn't go anywhere beyond the here and now, or to completely reassess his attitude to relationships if Ruby wanted more from him than a place in his bed.

He never thought he'd be in this position again, but if there was one person that could persuade him to open his heart, to risk it on a relationship, it would be Ruby. Regardless that she was the one woman who'd caused him to shut off that part of himself in the first place. When loving someone meant being afraid to lose them, and made him weak.

It was Ruby's turn to sigh. 'I don't know, Harrison. It seems too soon to be talking about the future when we've only just reconciled the past.'

'I guess I'm just asking if this is a one-time deal?'

With her fingers tracing circles across his chest she looked up at him coquettishly. 'I hope not.'

'So...'

'So, I'm not ready for anything serious but I'm enjoying this.' She reached up and kissed him full on the mouth. There was no arguing with her logic. By not putting a label on the nature of their relationship, it removed some of the fear of getting involved with her again. There was no pressure of commitment, of having to open up completely. Tentatively getting to know one another and being part of one another's lives again gave them permission to be together without promising forever. It was only natural that they should both be cautious this time around when the past had been so painful.

'Me too.' Harrison wrapped his arms around her, relishing the skin contact that reminded every part of him that Ruby was back in his life.

Ruby laid her head on Harrison's chest with a contented smile on her face, listening to the steady beat of his heart. A reassuring sound that always used to help her sleep, knowing he was there, making her feel safe. She wanted to feel that way again after years of being too afraid to give herself completely to another man.

There was no promise that Harrison would be in her life forever, but perhaps that was preferable to believing he would be, only for him to let her down. This was enough for now. This feeling of connection, of passion with a man who already knew her so well, was more than she'd had in a long time. If nothing else, perhaps having this chance to be together would eventually give them closure on the past. Something they both desperately seemed to need.

The revelation about his brother, his depression and subsequent withdrawal from her life were things they'd never had the opportunity to work through together. Some time together now might help them move forward. Whether that would be together was yet to be determined. Caution was called for even though she was keen to share his bed again. She wasn't ready for anyone to be a permanent fixture in her—or her daughter's—life, but Harrison was managing to help remove some of those barriers she'd built. Letting her believe for the first time in years that perhaps she wouldn't be alone for the rest of her days. That eventually she might find someone who loved her enough to stick around.

If she was willing to risk letting Harrison back in her life, she might find it easier to let others close in the future. As long as she didn't let him break her heart all over again.

Only time would tell if she was making a huge mistake by listening to her heart instead of her head.

CHAPTER NINE

'HOW ARE YOU FEELING?' Harrison asked Ruby as they passed one another in the hospital corridor.

The sight of him instantly made her smile, and want to crawl back into bed with him.

'Good. Tired.' Not that she was complaining. Her lack of sleep was a direct result of enjoying more of his sexual prowess between the sheets. Although it had meant for a frantic day at home trying to get everything done, and pick up Aimee from school to take to her mother's, all before she started another shift.

They'd been juggling their schedules for over a week now, trying to spend time together when they could. That had meant confiding in her mother too in order to get a babysitter when needed. Of course her mother wasn't happy that they'd rekindled their relationship, but Ruby had assured her it wasn't anything serious. Not that that detail had convinced her letting Harrison Blake back into their lives in any shape or form was a good idea.

Ruby was still a little wary herself. Although they were doing their best not to rush into anything serious, it felt as though they couldn't get enough of one another. Even now, just talking to him here she wanted to bundle him off into a private room and have her wicked way with him again. It was like being a teenager all over again. Heart beating quicker every time she thought of him, thoughts occupied by when she'd see him again. Dangerous territory she knew, but so intoxicating. That rush of blood in her veins, that excitement, was something she hadn't realised she needed in her life. She'd been so afraid of getting hurt, of messing things up at home for Aimee, Ruby had kept things safe. Predictable. Whilst she'd been comfortable with that routine, being with Harrison had reminded her there was more to life if she was willing to take a risk every now and then. She just hoped she didn't lose everything again because she'd put her faith and trust in those feelings. In the wrong man.

Harrison started to reach a hand out to her before snatching it away again. 'You know I really want to kiss you.'

'Me too,' she whispered. In line with keeping things casual, they didn't want any of their work colleagues to know there was anything going on between them. Plus, they still had to remain professional. It simply meant that desire kept bubbling away all day until they got to be alone. Making their quality time together all the more special.

'When am I going to have you to myself again?'

'I'm off tomorrow night if you are? I hear it's someone special's birthday…'

Harrison's eyes lit up as brightly as his smile. 'You remembered?'

'Of course.' She didn't tell him that she'd remembered every year since their split, and it had become a day of reflection and sadness for her. Hopefully this one would be different.

'I hadn't anything planned so maybe we could go out somewhere?' There was a hope in his eyes that she didn't want to dim, even though being seen out together was something they'd avoided so far.

Yes, they were being cautious. Overly, perhaps. With the fact they were sleeping together on a regular basis, going out shouldn't be such a big deal for them. Except perhaps that it was venturing out of the bedroom and into the real world. Which meant taking their relationship somewhere else. Deep down, Ruby knew that was what she wanted, she was simply too afraid to ask for it, or take that leap. For now, they'd have to take things one step at a time and hope things didn't blow up in their faces again.

'I'd like that. What about the prize you won at the casino? Maybe you could cash that in and we could make a proper night of it. Dinner, a night in a hotel…'

'Sold,' he said with a grin. 'I'll contact the casino and make arrangements, then we'll celebrate tomorrow.'

'Can't wait.' Ruby would be counting the hours until they could be together again, and praying the painful part of their history wouldn't repeat itself a second time.

Harrison couldn't remember the last time he felt this excited about a date, or his birthday. Neither were usually a particularly big deal to him, until tonight. This was different. He was getting to spend his birthday with Ruby, doing things that normal couples did. Of course, they hadn't put a name to their relationship status, but it seemed to be heading in that direction. Being a couple. He was beginning to realise that was what he wanted with her.

It was early days, but they had so much history already it was difficult not to get ahead of himself. There was still a lot for them to sort through, and he knew Ruby's life was complicated with Aimee. He couldn't just swan in and expect to be part of the family, even if he was ready for that, which he wasn't. Tonight was simply the first step out of their comfort zone. Testing the waters. Providing neither of them got too freaked out by going out as a couple, it could be the start of something new. A life he could share with someone.

The limo pulled up outside Ruby's apartment. He'd made the arrangements with the casino for their night and wanted to pick her up as though it were a proper date. Dressed to impress hopefully, he'd donned a suit and white dress shirt, and made his way to her front door carrying a bunch of red roses. Cliché, perhaps, but he owed her some tender loving care along with a smidge of romance.

When she opened the door he was almost lost for words at the sight. She was wearing a sleeveless silver sequinned minidress that showed off her fabulous legs, with a low-cut neck displaying her cleavage.

'Too much?' she asked, giving him a twirl.

'You look…amazing,' he managed to stutter eventually.

'These are for you.' He handed over the bouquet and she inhaled the scent.

'Thank you. I can't remember the last time anyone bought me flowers. I'll just put them in some water and grab my bag. Come on in.' She opened the door wider granting him access.

Harrison stepped into the hall to be greeted by Aimee, who threw herself at him. 'Hi, Harrison. Doesn't Mommy look pretty?'

'Yes, she does, Aimee. Very pretty.'

'Aimee, go back inside and finish your dinner.' Ruby's mother appeared wearing a cross expression, and Harrison suddenly felt like a nervous schoolboy.

'Hello again, Mrs Jones.'

'Don't you dare hurt her again.' It was all she said before turning and walking away, leaving Harrison calling after her.

'I won't. I swear.'

'What was all that about?' Ruby asked on her return, sensing the tense atmosphere between them.

'Me and your mother are just getting reacquainted. Now, are you all set for the night of your life?'

'That's a big promise,' she laughed as they made their way to the sleek black limousine provided for the evening.

'One I fully intend living up to,' Harrison whispered in her ear, feeling her tremble as he wrapped an arm around her waist.

They strapped themselves into the back seat and Harrison was able to show off all the extras which had been provided for them. At the push of a button music began to play, a disco ball began to spin and LED lights lit the interior of the vehicle.

'*Now* it's a party,' he said, pouring the bottle of champagne the casino had included and handing a glass to Ruby.

'Happy birthday.' She clinked her flute to his and he couldn't resist her for a second longer, leaning in for a kiss.

'I've been waiting to do that since yesterday,' he said, once they eventually broke apart.

Ruby leaned her forehead against his and he knew she'd been feeling the same way.

'So, where are we going?'

'I thought we could go to a drive-through chapel and get married.'

She narrowed her eyes at him. 'Not funny.'

'Sorry. I just thought we could do a tour of the strip. Be tourists for the night. Then we'll have dinner, a little wine and bed.' He kissed her neck, making his way slowly to the spot behind her ear he knew drove her insane.

'Sounds good.' Her breathy reply said they were both on the same page and their date was simply foreplay for the night they knew they were going to spend in bed together.

She leaned her head against his shoulder as they made their way along the strip. The bright lights and glitz of the world outside no competition for the feel-good factor of being here with Ruby.

They cruised along the main streets people-watching and enjoying the sights cuddled up together. Street performers entertaining them as well as the crowds with magic tricks and dance-offs. As much fun as it looked out there being part of the scene, he was happy being here in their little bubble. He didn't know how long this bliss could last. Experience had taught him not to get too lost in it, because when that bubble burst he ended up broken and alone. But it was hard not to wish this could be forever.

Suddenly, the car came to a sharp stop, almost sending them head first into the partition glass between them and the driver.

The chauffeur immediately lowered the glass to speak. 'Apologies, sir. There's an accident up ahead. We might have to sit here for some time.'

'Is anyone hurt?' he asked, but the driver couldn't see from his position exactly what had happened.

Harrison couldn't in good conscience sit here knowing someone could be hurt. 'I'm just going to take a look and see what's going on.'

He unclipped his seat belt only to find Ruby doing the same.

'What? You're not going without me. I'm the ER nurse, remember?'

She had a point and he wasn't going to start arguing when he knew she likely had more experience in this area than he ever would.

They stepped out onto the road where cars and crowds of people were creating obstacles to the scene of the accident. Harrison took Ruby's hand and guided her around the stationary vehicles until they reached the site where a man was lying prostate on the ground and a truck was half on the pavement, half on the road, the hood caved in. It didn't take a genius to work out it had hit a pedestrian.

'Are you okay to do this?' Ruby asked. Even though he'd only recently confided in her about his brother's death, she was already anticipating how triggering this scene could be for him. Thankfully, therapy and time had helped him to deal better with situations like this and he was able to compartmentalise to a certain degree so he could treat the patient in the moment. Of course, that didn't mean he wouldn't think of his brother at all, but at least he was able to function these days. It also helped having Ruby here with him, understanding how this could affect him and being there in a professional capacity to back him up too.

Harrison nodded. 'I'll check on the driver.'

'I'll take the pedestrian.'

They went their separate ways to check on both casualties while they waited for the paramedics to get here, in case anyone needed their immediate attention.

Harrison opened the cab door of the truck and the stench of alcohol filled his nostrils. He had to fight the rising swell of anger building inside to reach out to the driver.

'Sir, can you hear me? I'm a doctor. You've been in an accident. Can you tell me if you've been hurt?'

The man groaned and lifted his head from the steering wheel where it was resting.

'Sir? Can you hear me?' Harrison tried to look in the man's eyes as he had a head injury and he wanted to assess him for possible concussion, but the man batted him away.

'Leave me alone.' His words were slurred, his breath stinking of booze. In that situation it was difficult not to think about his brother, who'd been hit and left to die at the side of the road. It was likely by a drunk driver, though they'd never been identified to confirm that theory. This was another selfish man whose actions could have caused the death of another, but he still had to treat him the way he would any patient.

'Sir, you have a head injury. Possible concussion.' Harrison couldn't get close enough to examine the wound on the man's forehead, but at least he was conscious and talking, if belligerent.

'Get out of here.' The driver gave him a shove so he stumbled back.

At that point a police officer had arrived on scene so Harrison addressed him. 'I'm a doctor. I didn't see what happened but the driver appears to have a head injury. He's not being cooperative.'

'Thank you. I'll take it from here. The paramedics are on the way.' The officer would likely figure out for himself that he was dealing with a drunk driver and, reassured that his assistance was no longer required, Harrison went to help Ruby.

'Can I do anything to help?' he asked, kneeling down beside the injured pedestrian, where Ruby was hunched over the man.

'He's unconscious, unresponsive, breathing shallow, pulse weak.' As she relayed her assessment, the man suddenly began fitting.

Ruby worked quickly to undo the zipper of his hoodie to provide him some breathing room. Harrison stripped off his jacket and bundled it around the man's head. It was possible the fit was a direct result of his head hitting the pavement, and all they could do was wait until it subsided. Making sure that he wasn't in danger of swallowing his tongue or injuring himself further.

'Can you help me move him into the recovery position?' Ruby asked, once the man began to still again.

Between them they managed to roll him onto his side so he didn't choke if he vomited. Another police officer arrived bringing a first aid kit and a foil blanket to cover him with.

'Thanks,' Harrison said, accepting the offered items. 'We don't want to move him until the paramedics get here. They will stabilise him with a neck brace and back-board to prevent any further injury.'

'How bad are his injuries?'

'We won't know until he's had a CT scan but I think he's sustained a serious head injury.' Ruby was calm and clear as she conversed with the officer and in that moment Harrison was unbelievably proud of the woman she'd become.

More than that, he knew he was still in love with her. That was why he'd carried on seeing her, sleeping with her, and he couldn't fool himself any longer that this was merely some sort of casual fling. The question now was whether or not he was brave enough to act on his feelings this time. To be honest and put himself out there, regardless of the consequences.

* * *

'Hey, Wyatt.' Ruby greeted the paramedic, glad to be handing over responsibility of the scene.

His eyes widened at the sight of her. 'Wow. You scrub up well, Rubes.'

'Thank you.' Ruby blushed, and felt Harrison bristle beside her. There was no need for him to feel jealous but the fact that he did gave her a little thrill. Perhaps he wasn't as relaxed about their relationship as he suggested. She knew she wasn't. Although the night wasn't going as planned, it had proved to her that her feelings for her ex-husband weren't completely resigned to the past. He was back to being her safe place. The man she could cuddle up to, or who would back her up in a medical emergency. A risky turn of events when it was still so important that she protected herself from getting hurt again.

Once she and Harrison had given all relevant information and observations on the casualties, they made their way back to the limousine where the driver was clapping them for their assistance. Ruby was glad to get back into the anonymity of the blacked out car, away from the crowds and the pressure to be strong.

When Harrison closed the car door, she immediately curled up beside him on the back seat. 'I'm sorry your birthday didn't work out as planned.'

'It's not over yet.' He lifted the remainder of the bottle of champagne from the ice bucket and poured out another two glasses.

She grimaced as she looked down at her ruined dress covered in dirt and blood. 'I'm not sure I'm really dressed for dinner anymore.'

'Nor me. Maybe we can get room service instead.' Harrison sounded as weary as she felt. The adrenaline rush from the drama now leaving her body, so all that Ruby wanted to do now was crash out. Thank goodness they appeared to be on the same page. They always had been which was what had made them such a good team in the past.

'Sounds good.' She sipped at her champagne, though it was making her sleepy rather than fuelling her for a night on the town.

Once the ambulance had left the scene and the traffic began to move again, Harrison directed the driver to take them to the hotel where they had a suite waiting for them. He'd already checked in, so they were able to go on up to the penthouse in the elevator, bypassing too much public scrutiny of their bloodstained clothes.

The room was like nothing she'd ever seen before except on television. Marble floors, gold embossed wallpaper, and crystal chandeliers hanging from the high ceiling. Full-length windows all around gave a full view of the city lights below, with enough couches dotted around the vast space to accommodate an entourage.

'We could have a real party in here if you wanted.' She walked over to the bar area which was fully stocked with every drink imaginable. It seemed overkill for just the two of them.

Harrison grabbed hold of her and pulled her hard against his body. 'I prefer it being just us.'

He kissed her slowly and thoroughly until she was sure her legs were about to give way beneath her. Then Ruby took him by the hand and led him towards the master bedroom. A vast room dominated by the bed in the middle. Dark panelled walls, modern monochrome geometric patterned carpet and angular lamps made it into a sleek space. Not least because of the floor-to-ceiling windows.

'I wanted to let you unwrap your birthday present,' she said, stripping off her dress to reveal the sexy lingerie she'd bought specially for the occasion.

'Happy birthday to me,' Harrison growled before lunging towards her.

Ruby let out a squeal as she backed up onto the high bed. He kissed her and pushed her gently back onto the mattress, with his body fully covering hers. She heard his shoes drop to the floor as he kicked them off, and the rustle of his shirt as he pulled it out of his pants and over his head without unbuttoning it. The urgency he was showing to get naked with her was such a turn-on.

He kissed her all over, every touch a distraction from the thoughts in her head telling her she needed to know if he was going to commit to her. When Harrison was peeling away her underwear, tasting every part of her with his tongue, she didn't care about anything else.

There was a feverish need for one another she suspected had been ramped up by their restraint at work, and the adrenaline rush from the accident scene. So much so, neither of them seemed to want to take things slowly for once.

Harrison stripped away the rest of his clothes and only stopped to put on a condom before thrusting into her in one fluid movement to bring her instant satisfaction. She felt complete, content and happy. Then he began to move and elevated her into that now familiar state of bliss.

Life with Harrison had never been boring, always passionate and exciting, and that hadn't changed at least. Ruby knew she didn't want to be without him, or those feelings he elicited within her, for another day, never mind another fifteen years. They didn't have to move in together or remarry to cement their relationship status. All they had to do was take another chance on one another and try to get it right this time.

Harrison's climax came just as Ruby let go too, both giving themselves over to that overwhelming pleasure. He was able to lose himself with Ruby so easy it should have terrified him after spending years holding back from any sort of emotional attachment. Except he knew this was everything. Being with the woman who'd always had his heart.

'We didn't even close the window blinds,' she giggled as he lay down beside her.

'I think we were both too preoccupied to care, though I don't think anyone can see what we're getting up to here.' Despite potentially exposing themselves to the outside world, neither made a move to cover themselves. Apart from being on the top floor of the building, the room was dimly lit, and people were more likely paying attention to the fireworks going off outside rather than the ones inside the hotel room.

'Look, they've put on a show just for us.' Ruby spooned against his naked body in their increasingly familiar post-coital position. She wasn't always able to stay for the night because of Aimee and work obligations, so tonight made a pleasant change. Especially since his bed seemed so empty the moment she left.

'It's only fair since we put one on for everyone else,' he teased, earning himself a playful slap on the backside.

'I'm sorry we didn't get to celebrate your birthday the way we'd planned, Harrison.'

'I'm not complaining. Although I think I've worked up an appetite, along with a thirst. I'll call for room service once I've recovered the use of my limbs.' He didn't want to move at all, content to lie here with Ruby in his arms, but he would need sustenance when he planned to spend the night showing her just how he felt about her.

'Harrison?'

'Mmm?' He was doing his best not to drift off to sleep, though he was so comfortable and content it was a tough call.

Ruby twisted around so she was facing him, her breasts pressed tightly against his chest and helping to keep him awake.

'Do you think perhaps we should introduce you to Aimee as my partner, instead of just a friend?' She was worrying her bottom lip with her teeth, clearly anxious about raising the matter with him.

Harrison knew she wouldn't suggest it if she wasn't serious about being with him, and that meant moving their relationship into more permanent territory. Something they'd both said they didn't want, but he'd come to the conclusion it was all he wanted. He was glad Ruby had been seeing their time together as something special enough to move to the next stage. A huge deal for both of them, but given how well things had been going for them, not a huge surprise. It was a relief to know that he was more than a casual fling to her when being with her was the highlight of his day.

'Is that what you want?' That in itself was a big step. It meant a commitment to Aimee too, and a promise not to hurt either of them. Ruby knew that and she would never suggest such a thing if she wasn't putting her trust in him. After how their marriage had ended Harrison knew it was a leap of faith for her and he didn't want to let her, or Aimee, down. He just hoped he lived up to expectation.

'Only if you do. I don't want to pressure you into a commitment you're not ready for.'

'We can take it slowly. We don't want to cause Aimee a big upheaval. Why don't I just tag along on days out, or come over for dinner until she gets used to me?' A gentle introduction for all of them for a new dynamic. Having a family wasn't something he'd considered since they'd lost their baby, and being invited to join Ruby's felt like a huge responsibility. As much as he would like the fairy tale ending, he wanted some time to accept the new nature of their relationship too.

A challenge he was ready to meet if it meant having Ruby in his life permanently.

CHAPTER TEN

'HARRISON IS GOING to take us out for burger and fries, Aimee. Is that okay with you?' Ruby had waited until Harrison had arrived at the front door before sharing that information with her daughter. It was such a huge thing for her to introduce a man into Aimee's life, even if Harrison was already known to them both.

Since their night on the town a few weeks ago when they'd both voiced a desire to take their relationship to the next level Harrison had dropped by to watch a movie with them, or to have dinner. Just so Aimee got used to having him around before Ruby was upfront about the nature of their relationship.

She knew her mother didn't approve and that was only natural after she'd watched Ruby's suffering the first time she'd been with Harrison. Still, her parents were always there to babysit when she wanted to spend time with

Harrison and didn't try to interfere, and she respected them for that.

'Sure. Can we get milkshakes too?' Her daughter was more easily persuaded onboard. Ruby had always worried it would be too big of an upheaval introducing a male figure into their lives, or perhaps it had simply been a convenient excuse to keep everyone else at arm's length. Harrison was slotting into the family nicely. As though he was always meant to be part of it. That's what scared her. If something happened now, if he were to disappear out of their lives the way he had out of hers before, she'd be devastated all over again. An even greater loss now that they were becoming the family they were always supposed to have been, and she didn't want Aimee to go through the same heartbreak if he walked out on her too.

'If your mom says it's okay.' Harrison checked with her before agreeing to anything. He was learning. Setting boundaries in place so that Aimee didn't think she could wrap him around her little finger to get her own way. Since Harrison seemed equally as besotted with her as she was with him, there was a very good chance of that happening.

"Okay."

'Yay,' her daughter exclaimed at the answering nod. Aimee grabbed Ruby's hand, and Harrison's, swinging between them as they made their way to the car.

It was hard not to get carried away with this comfortable feeling of the three of them together, because it was perfect. Too perfect. Harrison had become such an integral part of her work life, family life and her love life, she couldn't imagine living without him again. She hoped she would never have to.

Once Aimee was strapped into the back seat, Ruby got into the passenger seat, with Harrison driving. This marked their first trip out as a trio. To anyone on the outside they would have looked like any other happy family and she hoped this was only the start. That there would be plenty more trips like this until they were all comfortable with that label. Safe in the knowledge that nothing was going to ruin it.

They drove to an old-fashioned diner on the outskirts of the neighbourhood. She wasn't sure who was more excited about lunch, Harrison or Aimee, by the way the two bounded in, chattering about what they were going to order. Ruby loved the casual, relaxed atmosphere of the family-friendly place, which was all red leather booths and chrome bar-stools. A proper '50s-style hang-out complete with black-and-white-chequered floor and waitresses wearing cute pink sweaters and poodle skirts.

'What can I get you folks?' The gum-chewing pony-tailed waitress asked once they'd had a chance to view the laminated menus.

'Can I have a cheeseburger, please?' Aimee asked, proud of herself for being able to order her own dinner. Tonight made all the more special because Ruby usually kept fast food to a minimum, preferring to cook fresh, wholesome food when she was home. It would be nice for the three of them to have dinner every night. Coming home to Harrison and even having someone to help her. Real teamwork.

'And Dad?' The question directed at Harrison seemed to throw him, colour infusing his cheeks. He glanced at Ruby, then Aimee, as though expecting them to get upset by the misunderstanding.

'I, er—'

'You said you were getting a cheeseburger and fries too,' Aimee prompted him without a hint of confusion or upset. She'd accepted Harrison so readily as part of her life that Ruby wondered if she'd been waiting, ready for her mother to find someone again. Or, just like her mother, perhaps Harrison made her feel safe and loved enough to let him into her life too.

'That's right, and strawberry milkshakes.' Harrison flashed Aimee a smile and in that second Ruby wished he were her real father. They already had a connection and she knew he'd protect Aimee with his life. More than her ex had managed.

'Mom?' the waitress asked, unaware of the significance of her mistake. Not one of them had taken umbrage or thought to correct her. The three of them knew Harrison wasn't Aimee's father but he was slowly fitting into that role so it hadn't seemed to matter that a stranger would assume it as fact.

'Make that three of everything.' Ruby handed over the menus and sat back, watching her daughter and her ex-husband chatting as though they'd known one another their whole lives.

When Harrison looked up and caught her watching him, the contented smile he gave her made Ruby's heart flip. She just hoped this picture-perfect life wasn't too good to be true.

'Do you have any plans for later this afternoon?' Harrison asked once they'd cleared their plates and filled their bellies.

'I'm all yours,' Ruby said with a grin, causing his body to stir with interest which he was forced to quell for now. Hopefully later, once Aimee was in bed, they'd be able to act on it. He was aware they needed to take things slowly in front of her and as hard as it was, he was exercising serious control. Not touching Ruby at all so they didn't draw the child's attention. So far Aimee had been going with the flow and hadn't raised any objection to him being more involved in their routine. However, that might change if she had any suspicion they were more than just work colleagues. He wasn't Aimee's father and couldn't expect to simply become part of the family overnight. Therefore any kissing, or even hugging, had to remain in private for the foreseeable future.

He wanted to get this right for everyone's sake, and that meant making sure Aimee was as comfortable with him being around as he was being with them.

'I thought we might go to the beach. Once our food gets down of course.' His surprise brought a gasp of delight from Aimee and a puzzled expression from Ruby.

'The beach? Isn't it going to be a little late to drive all the way to the beach?' she asked, understandably confused when they essentially lived out in the desert.

'When is a beach not a beach? When it's an artificial one created at a hotel. I've got passes for us to go and enjoy the afternoon there. There's a pool, a waterslide, sand, a beach bar…' This was all new to him. This feeling of having to prove himself extended not only to Ruby, but to Aimee as well. He wanted to be accepted, to be fun and someone they both looked forward to seeing.

His chance to be a father had been taken from him. Even his time as a brother and husband had been cut short, making relationships a difficult thing for him to navigate. Though he was willing to try. Regardless that planning happy family-oriented days out were beyond his comfort zone.

'I'm sold.' Now that he'd explained they wouldn't have to travel as far as expected Ruby looked as thrilled as Aimee, who was literally bouncing in her seat.

'Can I go home and get my swimsuit, Mom? Can I wear the blue one with the seahorses on it?'

'Of course. I'll have to go and get mine too. What about you, Harrison? Do you have anything suitable?' Ruby's eyes were glittering with mischief and he wondered if she was imagining him in his swimwear just as he was picturing her.

'I was going to wear my blue swimsuit with seahorses but I guess I'll have to pick something different now.' He gave an exaggerated sigh making Aimee laugh.

'You're so silly, Harrison. Can we go now?' Keen to start her adventure, Aimee was now out of her seat.

'I guess so.' As soon as he paid the cheque Aimee was out the door and waiting to get back into the car.

'You really do know how to keep a girl happy.' Ruby gave him a quick kiss on the cheek out of Aimee's sight before they joined her outside.

'I do my best,' he whispered in her ear, feeling triumphant when he felt her shiver.

Today was all about family time. Something he thought he'd never have and he was working hard to deserve, but tonight was going to be adult alone time, proving to Ruby how much he loved her.

'This is the life.' Ruby relaxed back into the sun lounger with a cocktail in hand. She looked beautiful in her black one-piece. Modest, but form-fitting enough to attract Harrison's attention. Aimee was in her element building sandcastles on the manmade beach nearby where they could keep an eye on her. So far, everyone seemed to be enjoying their day.

He was doing his best to get into the spirit of things, though fun family time had ceased in his life when his brother died. No one had the heart to even be together after that, never mind pretend they were enjoying life without him. There hadn't been much call for Harrison to be part of anything like this since. It was heartbreaking in a way, reminding him of when he was younger and he and Joey played on the beach together. However, it was also heartwarming knowing he was able to provide Aimee and Ruby with a nice day out and hopefully some good memories to hold on to. Like the ones he had with his family before their world fell apart.

'I could get used to this too,' he said, meaning being part of this with Ruby and Aimee, not necessarily just lounging around. It wouldn't matter if they were on a beach, or at home watching television on the couch, this was the happiest he'd been since his marriage had ended.

Ruby had always been his happy place. The person who'd moved him on from the grief of losing his brother without ever knowing it. They would never be able to replace the child they lost but Aimee was giving him so much joy she felt like family. He should have been terrified by the prospect of also becoming part of the little girl's life. The sort of responsibility he usually shied away from, but this all felt so right. As though it was always meant to be. He'd spent years wondering what kind of father he would have made and perhaps he'd finally be able to find out.

'Have you got sunscreen on?' Ruby asked, lowering her sunglasses to address him.

He shook his head feeling chastised as she tutted before reaching for the bottle of lotion in her bag. The magic bag which appeared to have everything anyone ever needed for a day at the beach. Towels, snacks, Band-Aids, all the essentials for a prepared mom. He'd always known Ruby would make a good mother, but he'd worried he wouldn't be up to the parenting job himself when his own hadn't been the greatest role models. There was a lot to learn but he hoped if he was going to become a father figure for Aimee he would be able to provide the sort of love and support his big brother had shown him.

Joey had been the substitute parent in his life and he would try and emulate him best he could, though Aimee and Ruby made it easy for him to love them. There was no doubt in his mind that was what he felt for them, otherwise he wouldn't be playing happy families like this, and revelling in every second of it.

Even now as he turned around so Ruby could apply the sunscreen, he was appreciating having someone who cared about him in his life. It had been such a long time, he'd forgotten how it felt. How even such a small gesture meant that someone was thinking about his welfare.

He considered himself extremely lucky to have been given a second chance not only as Ruby's partner, but perhaps as a father as well.

'Mom, can I go down the water slide?' Aimee appeared beside their sun loungers when the pool apparently became more attractive to her than the mounds of sand.

'Just be careful. And no running,' Ruby called after her as she hurried towards the covered flume which twisted and turned from a great height to drop the riders into the pool. They'd made sure to cover her burn and make it waterproof so she could fully enjoy the day out.

'Will she be all right?' Harrison couldn't help but worry. He didn't know how Ruby ever let her daughter out of her sight when he seemed to fret about her every move. He'd seen enough injuries in children, and seen their distraught parents, to know how easily accidents happened. Ruby was the parent, the expert, and he would have to follow her lead, but he doubted he'd ever stop worrying.

Ruby smiled. 'Relax. We can see her from here and she's a great swimmer. She's been taking lessons since she was a baby.'

That went some way to reassuring him. Along with the wave Aimee gave them as she ascended the steps. Both he and Ruby watched her, waving back, even though his heart was in his mouth once she climbed into the chute. When she plunged into the pool with a mighty splash he could hear her shriek of delight, and saw the big smile when she resurfaced, pushing the wet hair from her face.

He breathed a sigh of relief. Until she shouted over, 'I'm going again.'

Although he lay back again, he still watched her climb the steps and disappear into the chute. This time however, she seemed to be hurtling down faster than the last time and as she shot out the bottom, he heard a thunk as she hit her head on the slide before disappearing under the water.

When she didn't immediately reappear, Harrison leapt to his feet and ran towards the pool. He was vaguely aware of Ruby running behind him, and the sound of the lifeguard's whistle before he jumped in. He grabbed Aimee's seemingly lifeless body and swam over to the side of the pool where Ruby and the lifeguard managed to haul her out. By the time he climbed out Ruby had Aimee lying on her back and was making sure her airways were clear. She put her ear to her daughter's mouth and checked for her pulse.

'She's not breathing. Someone call the paramedics.'

Harrison could hear the fear quivering in her

voice and he took over to give Aimee rescue breaths. Delivering much-needed oxygen to her lungs. Tilting her head back to open her airway, pinching her nose shut and making a seal with his mouth over hers. He blew in gently, enough to make her chest rise, and repeated five times. Ruby checked her pulse again and shook her head, dislodging a torrent of tears, so Harrison began the chest compressions.

With one hand over the other, he pushed down on Aimee's chest hard and fast, alternating the compressions with rescue breaths. Eventually, she coughed up some water and Ruby cried out her relief as Harrison rolled her daughter into the recovery position in case she vomited.

'She's okay,' he told a sobbing Ruby before folding her into his arms.

They covered Aimee with towels provided by other swimmers and spectators and waited for the paramedics to arrive. Even though she seemed fine now it was important Aimee was checked over at the hospital in case of secondary drowning where the lungs could still fill with fluid. Someone handed him a blanket and regardless of the fact he was cold and wet, he wrapped it around Ruby's shaking shoulders.

'Hey, Rubes, how is she doing?' The paramedic she seemed to know arrived on scene with his medical bag.

'I think she's all right now but Harrison had to give her CPR,' she managed to get out through sobs.

'Okay, I'm just going to give her a quick check over here but we'll take her to the hospital just to be safe. I'm afraid I can only take one of you in the ambulance.' Both the paramedic and Ruby looked at him.

'Go. I'll pack up and follow you in the car.' Even though he wanted to accompany them, he wasn't Aimee's parent and had no rights. All he could do was watch helplessly as Aimee was stretchered off with Ruby walking alongside holding her daughter's hand.

It was only once they were out of sight he allowed himself to feel all the emotions which had been coursing through his body as he collapsed onto the sun lounger. That overwhelming panic he'd felt when she disappeared under the water wasn't just for her safety, but brought a lot of feelings he'd been trying to avoid for years. If they hadn't got her back, if they'd lost her the way they'd lost their baby, the way he'd lost Joey, it would have destroyed him all over again.

He was beginning to realise that fear as a parent, even a substitute one, was never going to leave him. Being part of a family meant being responsible for their safety, and unless he was watching Aimee twenty-four hours a day, he couldn't always ensure it. This was a prime example, and everything he'd feared.

It had been his choice for fifteen years not to be in this position. Feeling weak and helpless. Not getting close to anyone because of this very reason: the possibility of losing anyone else in his life. He'd chosen not to be a father, yet he was on the verge of making the decision to be part of Ruby and Aimee's family.

It was clear he couldn't be the partner, or father, they needed. Not at the cost of his own peace of mind. He hated to walk away again when they were on the verge of something good, but it was better he did it now than later when they were planning a future together again. Aimee had one fantastic mother in Ruby and he simply wasn't going to measure up to the parent role when his fear of losing them was preventing him from committing completely. Ruby and Aimee both deserved better than he could give them.

CHAPTER ELEVEN

'Hey. How's the patient?' The moment Harrison walked into her apartment Ruby just wanted to run and hug him. Not only had he saved her daughter's life, but his very presence made her feel safe. She didn't know when she'd stopped being the independent, bulletproof parent, but Ruby needed his comforting embrace to remind her that everything was all right. Even though Aimee had been home safe for several days.

'Good,' Aimee croaked from her makeshift bed on the sofa, her throat still sore from coughing. She'd been kept in hospital overnight for observation after the incident at the pool, while Ruby slept next to her in a chair, checking her breathing every few minutes. Thankfully she hadn't suffered any lasting damage.

It had been one of the most harrowing days of Ruby's life when she'd nearly lost another child. It was no wonder Harrison looked pale when he was probably still as shaken by the events as she was.

'I brought you some groceries and a few comics and candy for Aimee. I'm sure you haven't had a moment to get food in.' He handed over the grocery bag, a thoughtful gesture in keeping with the man Ruby knew, but there was something awkward in the interaction, as though he couldn't wait to get out of the place.

'Thanks. Is everything okay, Harrison?' He'd been a little distant these past couple of days. Although he'd remained in contact, he'd been quiet on the phone and there was just something about his antsy demeanour that immediately put her on high alert.

'Can I talk to you for a moment, Ruby?' He gestured that he wanted to speak to her in private, out of Aimee's earshot, and that fear that something was wrong took a greater hold.

She followed him out into the hall and closed the door behind her, a growing sense of dread curling up from her stomach. 'What's up?'

'Look, there's no easy way of saying this...' He was squirming, trying to find the words she had a feeling were coming, but she wasn't going to make it easy for him. If he was going to break her heart again, this time she wanted him to face her as he said the words.

'I just don't think this is going to work.'

'Why not?' She couldn't believe he was doing this after he'd convinced her he was always going to be there for her and Aimee. Literally saving her daughter's life and making her believe that he was committed to both of them.

'I'm just not cut out to be a parent. I know we're not there yet in our relationship, and perhaps that's a good thing so we can end this now, but you and Aimee need someone strong and fearless. That's not me.'

'What are you talking about? You jumped in to save Aimee without a second thought. You brought her back to life before my eyes. I don't understand why you think that you're not up to the job.'

He scrubbed his hands through his hair. 'Okay, to be more precise, I'm not ready for this level of commitment. Yes, I want to be with you, Ruby, but I can't do this. I thought perhaps given time after the accident I might feel a little differently, but I don't. Having some space has only confirmed to me that I'm not the man you need in your life. You deserve someone who won't spend every day worrying that something is going to happen to you or Aimee and wonder how he'll get through it. It's not good for any of us. I'm sorry but I can't lose anyone else.'

'Except me, apparently.' Ruby was almost doubled over in pain as he twisted the knife.

She'd thought it would be better to have an explanation but this didn't make her feel any better knowing there was nothing she could do. Aimee was her daughter and would always come first, but she'd let Harrison into her life because she'd believed him when he said he wanted to be part of it. That included being there for her daughter.

'Trust me, I don't want to walk away from you again, but I think it's the best thing for everyone for me to go now rather than in the future. At least Aimee won't know any different.'

It was a blessing that they hadn't declared their relationship status but Ruby knew her daughter would feel the loss just as she did, if not the anger along with it. He was taking the coward's way out. Instead of facing his fears, believing that being with them was more important than his illogical reason for leaving.

Ruby did know better. She knew what it was to go to bed at night with him, wake up in the morning and know he was going to be there for her no matter what. At least that was what she'd believed until this very moment.

'This is really what you want, Harrison? To give up on us because something might happen? Children get sick, they get hurt, just as we all do. It's a fact of life. As parents all we can do is our best to keep them safe, and as the accident at the pool proved, with two of us being medical professionals we can do that job better than most.'

Worrying about her daughter was simply part of her life. Unlike Harrison, she couldn't just decide she didn't want to do that anymore. It was how she showed she cared. Harrison was proving the opposite.

'But I'm not her father, am I?' And there it was in a nutshell. He didn't want the responsibility, and that left no room for compromise. She wasn't going to let him, or anyone else, into her life who couldn't make room for her daughter.

'No. You're not.'

'I'm never going to be and she deserves someone who can be strong for her no matter what. As you do.'

'You don't need to make excuses. As you've pointed out, you have no responsibility towards either of us so you're free to leave anytime you like, Harrison.' If getting her permission to go this time would make him feel better, that was on his conscience, not hers. She shouldn't have to persuade someone to love her enough to try and make things work. It was her fault for thinking he'd changed. At the first sign of trouble he was gone, again.

'I'm sorry, Ruby. I really am.' It didn't matter that he looked as upset as she felt when he was the one causing the pain. He might have saved her daughter's life but he was killing her.

She'd bought into the idea of the family he'd sold her, and he'd let her down for a second time. He was overreacting to something he had no power over. Ruby would never have sacrificed the chance to be a parent, to have a family, simply because she was scared.

Of course she understood to some extent why he didn't want to fully invest in a relationship with her and Aimee after all the loss he'd suffered, but he couldn't feel strongly enough for her if he wasn't even going to try and work through his issues. That wasn't someone she or Aimee needed in their lives. From now on it would be back to just being the two of them again because they couldn't rely on anyone else.

'Just go, Harrison. I wish you'd never come back into my life.' It wasn't true of course. These past weeks had been the happiest time of her life in years, but now it was coming at the ultimate price. A broken heart. The pain so immense she couldn't help but lash out. Harrison's wounded look as he walked away giving her some sense of justice that he might feel as dreadful in this moment as she did.

Ruby wanted to cry and rage at the injustice of it all, just as she had the last time he'd given up on them, but she had a daughter to take care of this time. Aimee's welfare took priority over everything. Even her mother's breaking heart.

'Breakfast is ready, Harrison.' The wake-up call from his mother rang from downstairs and for a brief moment he was transported back to his childhood. The smell of bacon and pancakes filling the house and rousing him and Joey from their beds. Except his brother wasn't here and he wasn't a kid anymore. He was a grown man hiding from his problems. A pattern he hadn't quite grown out of.

After leaving Ruby and Aimee he'd taken some time off work and with nowhere else to go, no one else to turn to, he'd contacted his mother. She'd been surprisingly happy to hear from him and had told him he could stay as long as he wanted to. Taking a couple of weeks off hadn't been a problem as holidays weren't something he took regularly. It had made him realise that until Ruby and Aimee had come into his life he hadn't spent a lot of time with anyone outside of work, and likely wouldn't again.

Although his mom had provided him with refuge she still had to work, so when they weren't out for a coffee together or making dinner, he was often left alone with his thoughts. It wasn't helping his mood. He had hoped coming here, dealing with a different difficult relationship would distract him from thoughts of Ruby, but in that respect, his trip had been a failure. In other areas, however, this visit home had been a success. His relationship with his mother recovering more with every day they spent together.

He got out of bed and pulled on a pair of pants before joining her in the kitchen. 'Morning.'

'Morning, sleepy-head. I thought you were never going to get out of bed. It's like having a teenager in the house all over again.' His mother joined him at the table she had laden with food. It was nice having someone to fuss over him when he thought he would never have that again after walking out on Ruby.

'We didn't always get to have breakfast together though. This is nice.' He reached for the maple syrup to pour on the stack of pancakes his mother had lovingly cooked for him before tucking in.

His mother set down her knife and fork, a sudden look of sadness on her face. 'I'm sorry your father and I weren't always there for you, Harrison.'

His fork stopped midway to his mouth with shock. 'It's okay. I know you were both working hard to provide for the family.'

'I mean after your brother died. We weren't there emotionally for you then, or when you lost your own baby. I'm so sorry. It brought back a lot of the emotions for me about losing Joey and it was easier for me to back away completely than to face my grief as well as yours.' Something he knew about. It seemed perhaps he'd taken his lead from his parents' way of dealing—or not—with emotions.

'I understand that, Mom. I haven't found it easy myself.'

Her face eased into a smile. 'Don't you think I've noticed that? Why do you think I'm telling you this now. I don't want you to make the same mistakes I did. Perhaps if your father and I had talked more about what we were going through after Joey died, or been there for you, we could have saved our family.'

Harrison nodded. He appreciated that she was recognising how difficult that time had been for him too. Even more that she was trying to make amends. He put down his cutlery and reached across the table to take her hand. 'We still can.'

Although his father wasn't in the picture anymore they could still have a family with just the two of them. Infinitely better than a future alone.

His mother took his other hand and drew

them towards her, forcing him to look at her. 'I'm not talking about just us, Harrison. We should have had this talk the first time your relationship broke down with Ruby but I wasn't in the right headspace then. I let you walk away from that marriage to lick your wounds whilst I dealt with mine. Now we're both older, with more life experience, I hope you'll listen to what I have to say. Does she make you happy?'

'She does.' At least until he'd ended things and every time he thought about her now he was overcome with sadness.

Until now he and his mother had avoided talking about why he'd come here. All he had told her was that he and Ruby had briefly reunited but had ultimately ended things for good. Perhaps now that he and his mother were making roads in their own relationship she thought it was safe to talk about the other one he'd let disintegrate.

'Then why did you leave her?' It was a simple enough question but not one he could answer easily.

He let go of her hands and sat back in his seat, suddenly feeling defensive. 'Because I love her too much.'

His mother gave a half-smile. 'I'm not trying to tell you what to do, Harrison, but don't make the same mistakes I did. Talk to her. Whatever is wrong I'm sure you can fix it. If you want to be with her don't let fear get in the way.'

'It's not that easy, Mom. I can't seem to get past the fact that I might lose her, or Aimee. I struggled so much after Joey died, then when we lost the baby, I know I couldn't go through that again.'

'There's nobody who understands that better than I do, Harrison, but look where it's got me. Alone, and until this week, estranged from everyone I love. I don't want you to end up like me.' She looked so sad Harrison just wanted to hug her. He wondered if he would be doomed to wear that same forlorn expression for the rest of his days too.

The whole point of walking away from Ruby and Aimee was to prevent further pain, from being depressed and miserable and unable to function. Yet, that was exactly what he was now. He wasn't any happier now having ended things and no longer having to worry about anyone's safety other than his own.

'You can't hide away here forever, Harrison. One day you're going to have to decide what it is you really want and fight for it.'

His mother's words struck a chord. Hiding was exactly what he was doing. Just as he had back then. Avoiding the reality of his feelings, afraid to deal with them. He'd spent these past years trying to forget Ruby, living a life of solitude and pretending it made him happy. When, in reality, he knew the only thing that could do that was being with her. He didn't want to spend another fifteen years regretting his actions. At least if he took the chance of being with her there was a possibility he might be happy again.

Except he'd already had his second chance with Ruby and he'd blown it. He doubted she'd let him back into her life for a third time.

'What if Ruby doesn't want me back?' Harrison knew his mother couldn't predict what would happen any more than he could, but at least he was voicing his fears. Even considering returning, speaking to her, wanting to try again was a step forward. Hopefully, that meant there was a chance he had the potential to be the man Ruby and Aimee deserved in their lives.

'That's a risk you have to take, otherwise you're going to lose her forever. Is that something you're prepared for?'

His mother's words made him stop and consider a world without Ruby. Something which seemed incomprehensible. Even a week without seeing or talking to her, she'd been constantly on his mind. How would he survive the rest of his life like that? Especially when he'd had a glimpse of the life available to him with her and Aimee, as a family?

Yes, he was always going to worry, be afraid of losing them, but perhaps that was simply part of loving someone. A symptom he could learn to live with if it meant having Ruby in his life.

With Aimee in bed and work over for the day, Ruby settled down onto the couch in her pyjamas with a glass of wine in her hand. It had been a tough week for all manner of reasons. Not only were they both haunted by what had happened at the pool that day, but losing Harrison had been difficult for them both. Aimee was missing him, asking where he'd gone, and why he was no longer coming around for dinner. Believing it was her fault for getting into trouble in the water and upsetting him, Ruby had to tell her that Harrison had gone away. He wouldn't be coming around anymore.

Unsurprisingly Aimee had been just as confused and upset as her mother by his sudden disappearance from their lives, but Ruby knew they had no choice but to move on. It would take time but she'd done it before and she had to do it again for her daughter's sake. Even if it hurt like hell.

There was a knock on the door, but she was hesitant to answer it at this hour of the night. She knew her parents would have phoned before turning up and she wasn't about to open the door in her nightwear, so she ignored it.

The second knock was followed by the sound of Harrison's voice. 'Ruby, can we talk?'

She sat up so quickly she almost knocked her wine all over herself. He was the last person she expected to call at her door and she was curious as to what had brought him here.

Ruby set down her glass and went to answer the door, opening it just a fraction. 'What are you doing here, Harrison?'

'I want to talk to you.'

'I thought we'd said everything that needed saying.' She hadn't. She hadn't told him how much she'd loved him, how much he was breaking her heart by leaving again, but it was the last bit of control she'd had by refusing to admit any of that.

'I've had some time to think.' He looked tired, not his usual groomed self, with stubble lining his jaw and his hair unkempt. Although, nonetheless sexy.

'And what?' Ruby folded her arms across her chest as if it was somehow going to prevent him from hurting her again even though she knew it was futile.

'Please, can I come in? Just let me say what I need to and if you want me to leave and never come back I will.' There was a plea in his eyes as well as his voice for her to hear him out and it touched her deep inside. Clearly he had something on his conscience and regardless of what had gone on, she didn't want to see him in pain, or be the cause of it.

She opened the door and walked back into the apartment, letting him follow behind.

'I heard you'd taken some leave.'

'I went to see my Mom for a few days.'

She was surprised to hear that when they'd never seemed especially close. Although Mrs Blake had been her mother-in-law, they'd only met on a couple of occasions, including on their wedding day.

'How did that go?'

'Good.' He gave a half-smile. 'Really good. We talked for the first time ever about the important stuff. About Joey, and the fact that none of us ever properly dealt with our grief. I'm hoping we can get our relationship back on track.'

She was genuinely pleased for him. He deserved to have family around him. Ruby didn't know how she would cope without Aimee or her parents. Especially now in the wake of their break-up. It was always good to know she had emotional support when she needed it. People she loved, and who loved her in return. He deserved to have someone like that in his life even if it wasn't her.

'I'm pleased for you. Is that all you came here to tell me?' If so, it was unbelievably cruel to turn up on her doorstep looking all rugged and sexy just to tell her he was happy when she was miserable without him.

'No. It made me think about us. About what I'd let slip through my fingers.'

Ruby hated that her heart quickened at that one glimmer of hope that all might not be lost. Even after all the hurt, Harrison Blake still made her love him and believe that he was the road to happiness.

She didn't speak, preferring to let him say what he'd come to say before she made any admission about how much she'd missed him.

'I'm sorry for leaving. *Again.* I was just so overwhelmed by my feelings for you, and Aimee, that it terrified me. I thought it would be easier to not have you in my life at all rather than love you and run the risk of losing either of you. I was wrong.'

'What do you want from me, Harrison?' It was a plaintive cry straight from her heart. A need to know where she stood once and for all, because having and losing him time and again was killing her.

'Another chance. I know I don't deserve it. You already gave me another chance and I failed you, but I couldn't do it this time. I couldn't just walk away and never see you again. I want to be with you, Ruby. I'm sorry. Please forgive me.'

It was a big ask, and as much as she wanted Harrison, and what they had together, she had to protect Aimee as well as herself.

'How do I know you're not going to leave again?' She'd gone against every instinct and let him into her life before only to regret it. To do it a third time would be welcoming more pain with open arms. As much as she loved him, at some point she had to love herself more.

He gave a heavy sigh. 'I don't know how to convince you. I can only tell you how much I love you. How you and Aimee mean the world to me, and I promise to do everything I can to make this work. To make you believe in us.'

'I always believed in us. It was you who never did.' She saw him flinch but it was true. Harrison hadn't stayed to fight for their relationship. At least this time he'd come back. He was doing what she'd wanted him to do then and opened up to her. Showed he still wanted her by turning up here tonight and exposing his heart instead of taking the easy way out.

Now it was down to her whether or not she was brave enough to do the same. She thought of the days and nights they'd spent together. The family picture they'd made together with Aimee, and how happy they'd been. How happy they could be. Ruby owed it to herself to grab hold of the possibilities instead of the painful past.

'It wasn't that I didn't believe in us, it was that I didn't believe in happy-ever-afters, but I know now that's something that isn't promised to anyone. All we can do is our best to make one another happy and I'm committed to doing that for you and Aimee. If you'll let me?' She saw the hope written in his face for a future together as a family. Something he'd been too afraid to show before, and it helped persuade her that he was worth another chance.

'Show me.'

'Pardon?' He frowned, clearly not understanding what she was asking of him.

'Show me how you're going to make me happy. How much you love me.' She smiled, letting him see that she was committed to giving him another chance to prove himself.

Harrison grinned and closed the space between them to take her in his arms. He kissed her full on the lips, taking his time to seduce her mouth with his firm but tender touch until arousal robbed her of coherent thought.

'Convinced yet?' he asked when they finally broke apart.

'Yes, but keep going.' Ruby wrapped her

arms around his neck and submitted to her desire, her passion and her love for the only man who'd ever had a claim on her heart.

EPILOGUE

'You may now kiss your bride.' The registrar gave Harrison permission to kiss Ruby. Something he would never grow tired of doing.

He swept her into his arms and kissed her fully, almost forgetting they had a small audience. Along with their bridesmaid, Aimee, Ruby's parents and his mother were in attendance to see them tie the knot for a second time.

He'd proposed only a month after she'd given him another chance to prove his love to her. It seemed pointless to wait when they already knew one another so well and he'd wanted to start their life together as soon as possible. Thankfully Aimee had been over the moon when she found out about their relationship, even if Ruby's parents had been a little harder to win over. He appreciated the fact they were here giving their support and making the day complete.

It was only when their guests began to clap that he remembered they weren't alone.

'Well, Mrs Blake, I guess we've done it again,' he said, taking her hand in his.

'This time it's forever.' It wasn't a question, it was a statement Ruby made, confirming her trust in him and he was grateful for it.

'I have one last gift for you.' He reached across and took Aimee's hand, bringing her over to join them at the front of the small gathering. She looked as pretty as her mom, dressed in a matching ivory silk shift dress but with a baby-pink sash tied around her waist which complemented his grey suit and pink pocket square.

'But you've already given us both so much.' Ruby touched the silver locket he'd gifted to her this morning, which carried a family photograph of the three of them together. He'd bought Aimee one too since it felt as though he was marrying both of them today. Even though they were already living together in his house, today marked their official commitment. There was just one more thing he wanted to do to prove he was devoted to their family.

'With Aimee's and your permission, I would like to officially adopt Aimee. If that's what you want of course?' At the last second his confidence wavered that he might be overstepping again. That they might not want him to claim any rights as her father even though that was definitely the role he wanted. It had come easier than he'd expected and he cherished every moment of having her in his life.

He shouldn't have worried. The second he said it, he found himself swamped in hugs with Ruby's arms around his neck, and Aimee's around his waist.

'Of course that's what we want, isn't it Aimee?' A teary Ruby looked to her daughter, who was nodding enthusiastically and bringing a lump to Harrison's throat.

'In that case, I think we should let the celebrations begin!' He took the hands of the two most important women in his life and led them down the aisle to another round of applause and tears. Ready to begin their new life together.

The family he hadn't realised he needed until Ruby and Aimee had crashed into his life. Lifting him out of the darkness and making his world so much brighter.

* * * * *

Look out for the next story in
the Sin City Nurses duet

Coming soon!

And if you enjoyed this story, check out these
other great reads from Karin Baine

A Nurse, a Pup, a Second Chance
Winter Nights with the Midwife
Spanish Doc to Heal Her

All available now!